Raves For the Work of
CHARLES WILLIAMS!

"A superb story of peril, suspense, and unexpected terrors…Brilliant, breathtaking, spectacular."
—*The New York Times*

"Charles Williams was Hemingway with grit in his teeth. He is one of the neglected hardboiled geniuses of his era, or any other era. His novels were perfect little gems."
—*Joe R. Lansdale*

"First-rate."
—*The New Yorker*

"A real pleasure to read…filled with danger and action and told with clarity."
—*San Francisco Chronicle*

"Something to marvel at. A-plus."
—*Columbus Dispatch*

"No one can make violence seem more real."
—*John D. MacDonald*

"[One] of the most adroit plot-spinners of the paperback era."
—*Geoffrey O'Brien*, Hardboiled America

I was lying stretched out on the sofa with that awful feeling of having been awakened by some tiny sound. I jerked my head up and looked groggily around the room, not seeing her at first.

Then I did.

She was slipping silently out into the hallway from the bedroom. She had on that nylon robe, with nothing under it, and she was carrying the scissors in her hand. She was barefoot. She took another soft step and then she saw me looking at her.

I couldn't say anything or move.

She saw me staring at the scissors. She put up a hand and patted the curls that gleamed softly in the light from the single lamp. I sat up. I still couldn't find my voice. Or take my eyes from the long, slender blades of those scissors.

She came on into the room and sat down on the floor with her back against the big chair across from me. I watched her with horror. She calmly lit a cigarette and leaned back against the chair doubling her legs under her. She paid no attention to the fact that she had on nothing under that flimsy robe.

"It's nice here, isn't it?" she said quietly.

Somewhere deep inside me I could feel myself beginning to come unstuck. She opened the scissors, playing with them in her hands. She balanced one slender, shining blade on her fingertip, like a child enchanted with some new toy, and looked from it to me and smiled. Light flickered and gleamed along the blades. Smoke from the cigarette in her hand curled upward around the wicked and tapering steel.

It wasn't that I was afraid of a 125-pound woman with a pair of drugstore scissors in her hand. It was that she wasn't human. She was invulnerable. She was unbeatable. Nothing could touch her...

**OTHER HARD CASE CRIME BOOKS
YOU WILL ENJOY:**

GRIFTER'S GAME *by Lawrence Block*
FADE TO BLONDE *by Max Phillips*
TOP OF THE HEAP *by Erle Stanley Gardner*
LITTLE GIRL LOST *by Richard Aleas*
TWO FOR THE MONEY *by Max Allan Collins*
THE CONFESSION *by Domenic Stansberry*
HOME IS THE SAILOR *by Day Keene*
KISS HER GOODBYE *by Allan Guthrie*
361 *by Donald E. Westlake*
PLUNDER OF THE SUN *by David Dodge*
BRANDED WOMAN *by Wade Miller*
DUTCH UNCLE *by Peter Pavia*
THE COLORADO KID *by Stephen King*
THE GIRL WITH THE LONG GREEN HEART
by Lawrence Block
THE GUTTER AND THE GRAVE *by Ed McBain*
NIGHT WALKER *by Donald Hamilton*

A TOUCH
of DEATH

by Charles Williams

A HARD CASE CRIME NOVEL

A HARD CASE CRIME BOOK
(HCC-017)
February 2006

Published by

Dorchester Publishing Co., Inc.
200 Madison Avenue
New York, NY 10016

in collaboration with Winterfall LLC

ISBN 0-8439-5588-0

The name "Hard Case Crime" and the Hard Case Crime logo
are trademarks of Winterfall LLC. Hard Case Crime books are
selected and edited by Charles Ardai.

Printed in the United States of America

Visit us on the web at www.HardCaseCrime.com

A TOUCH OF DEATH

Chapter One

It was a fourplex out near the beach. I stopped the car, looked at the ad again, and went up the walk. Only two of the mailboxes had names on them, and neither was the one I wanted.

This was the right address, though, so it had to be one of the others. I picked one at random and pressed the buzzer. Nothing happened. I tried again, and could hear it faintly somewhere on the second floor.

I waited a minute or two and tried the other. No one answered. I lit a cigarette and turned to look along the street. It was very quiet in the hot afternoon sun. A few cars went past on the sea wall, and far out in the Gulf a shrimp boat crawled like a fly across a mirror.

I swore under my breath. It had looked like a good lead, and I hated to give up. Maybe one of the other tenants would know where he was. I tried the buzzer marked Sorenson first, and when it came up nothing I leaned on the one that said James.

The whole place was as silent as the grave.

I shrugged and went back down the walk. I was about to get into the car when I saw the patio wall in the rear of the place. A walk ran past the side of the building to a high wooden gate, which was closed. There might be somebody back there. I stepped across the front lawn and went back to the gate and opened it.

"Oh. Excuse me," I said.

The girl was a brunette and she was sunbathing in the bottom part of a two-fragment bathing suit. She was lying face down on a long beach towel with a bottle of suntan lotion beside her and a book open in front of her on the grass. She turned her head casually and looked at me through dark glasses.

"Were you looking for someone?" she asked.

"Man named Winlock," I said. "He gave this address. Do you happen to know if he's around?"

"I'm new here," she said. "But I think the people in the other upstairs apartment are named Winlock or Winchester, or something like that. I suppose you tried the buzzer?"

"Yes. No dice."

She shrugged a satiny shoulder. "They may have gone out on a boat. I think he fishes."

"Oh," I said. "Well. Thanks a lot."

I started to turn away, and noticed she was staring at my face. Or at least I felt she was. The glasses were so dark I couldn't see what her eyes were doing.

"You could leave a note under the door," she said. "I think it's the third one from the left."

"Thanks," I said. "But I'm probably too late. I mean, since he's not home. The ad was in yesterday's paper."

"Ad?"

"He wanted to buy a late-model car."

"Oh."

She lay with her face turned toward me, her cheek

down against the towel, very relaxed but still watching me. The brassiere part of the bathing suit was under her, but she had untied the strap across the back. Tall, I thought, if she stood up. Not that she was likely to, with that thing untied.

"It sounds like a funny way to buy a car," she said.

"Lots of people do it," I said. "Saves a dealer's commission."

"I see. And you've got one for sale?"

"Yes."

"You're not a dealer?"

"No," I said. I wondered what she was driving at. The cigarette in my hand was burning short. I turned and tossed it through the gate onto the walk.

When I looked back she was working the strap of the halter gizmo up between her arm and side. She clamped it there and started to turn on her side, facing me, until it became obvious to both of us that the thing wasn't big enough to allow any leeway if she didn't have it straight. It was missing the mark. And there was quite a bit of it to miss.

"Would you mind?" she asked calmly. "Just for a moment."

"Oh," I said. "Sure." I turned and stared out the gate, but I could still see her in my mind. I'd called her a girl, but she was probably near thirty.

In a moment she said, "All right," and I turned around. She was sitting up on the towel with the long legs doubled under her. The halter was tied.

"What kind of car is it?" she asked.

"Fifty-three Pontiac. About fourteen thousand miles on it." I wondered again what was on her mind.

"How much do you want for it?"

"Twenty-five hundred," I said. "Why? You know somebody in the market for one?"

"Wel-l-l," she said slowly, "I might be. I've been thinking of buying a car."

"You could go farther and do worse," I said. "It's a two-tone job, white sidewalls, radio, seat covers—"

She was studying my face again with that curious intensity. "Is it worth twenty-five hundred dollars, really?"

"Every nickel of it," I said, ready to go into a sales pitch. Maybe we could make a deal. Then I got the impression that she wasn't even listening to what I said.

She took off the glasses and stared thoughtfully at me. Her eyes were large and self-possessed, and jet black, like her hair. The hair was long, drawn into a roll at the back of her neck. She looked Spanish, except that even with the faint tan her skin was very fair.

"There's something about your face," she said. "I keep thinking I should know who you are."

So that was it. It still happens once in a while. "Not unless you've got a long memory," I said.

She shook her head. "Not too long. Four years? Five?"

"Make it six."

"Yes. That's about it. I was quite a football fan in those days. Scarborough, wasn't it? Lee Scarborough? All-Conference left half."

"You should be a cop," I said.

"No. You were quite famous."

"They get new ones every year." I wished we could

get back to the car trade. You can't eat six-year-old football scores.

"Why didn't you join the pros?" She took a puff on the cigarette she was smoking and tossed it into a flower bed without taking her eyes from my face.

"I did," I said. "But it didn't jell."

"What happened?"

"Bum knee." I squatted on my heels. "How about the car? You really want to buy one?"

"I think so. But why do you want to sell it?"

"I need the money."

"Oh," she said.

"It's out front, if you'd like to drive it."

"All right," she said. "But I'd have to change. Would you mind?"

"Not at all. I'll wait in the car."

"Oh, come on up. It's cooler inside."

"O.K.," I said. We stood up. She was tall, all right. I picked up the suntan lotion and the book and towel.

"I'm Diana James," she said.

She saw me glance down at her left hand, and smiled. "You'll only have to make one sales talk. I'm not married."

"I'd have given you odds the other way."

"I was, once. But, as you say, it didn't jell."

We went up the outside stairs at the rear of the building and in through the kitchen. She pulled a bottle of bourbon out of a cupboard and set it on the drain.

"Mix yourself a drink, and go into the living room. Soda and ice cubes in the refrigerator."

"I hate to drink alone this early in the day," I said. "It scares me."

She smiled. "All right. If you insist."

I mixed two and handed her one. We went on through to the living room, looking out over the Gulf. She took a sip of her drink and put it on the coffee table.

"Just make yourself at home," she said. "I think this month's *True* is in the rack there. I won't be long."

I watched her walk back across the dining room to the short hall that led to the bedroom and bath. It seemed to take her a long time.

The car, I thought. Remember? Don't louse it up.

I sat down and glanced around the room. It had the anonymous look of any furnished apartment, but it wasn't cheap. Hundred or a hundred and fifty a week during the season, I thought. It was odd she didn't already have a car, and that, not having one, she wanted to buy a secondhand one.

Her purse was on the table at the end of the couch. I glanced at it, thinking she must be careless as hell or convinced all ex-football players were honest, and then I shrugged and started to take another sip of my drink. I stopped, and my eyes jerked back to the table.

It wasn't the purse. It was the alligator key case lying beside it. The zipper was open and the keys dangled loose on the glass. And one of them was that square-shouldered shape you recognize anywhere. It was the ignition key to a General Motors car. Just who was kidding whom?

Well, I thought, she didn't say she *didn't* have one. Maybe she wanted two, or she was selling the other one. It was her business.

When she came out she had on a short-sleeved white summer dress and gilt sandals without stockings. She was tall and cool and very easy on the eye. Taking another sip of the drink she'd left, she gathered up the purse and keys and we went out to the car. She slid in behind the wheel.

I was deliberately slow in handing her the keys to it, and she did just what I thought she'd do. She opened the alligator case and started to stab at the dash with her own. She caught herself, and glanced quickly at me. I didn't say anything, but I was beginning to wonder. She was trying to cover up the fact that she already had a car. Why?

We cruised to the end of the sea wall and out the beach, not saying much at first. The sand was firm, and when we began to get clear of the traffic and the suntan crowd she let it out a little, to around fifty-five.

"It handles nicely," she said.

"You're a good driver." I lit two cigarettes and handed her one.

"What do you do, Mr. Scarborough?" she asked, keeping her eyes on the beach ahead.

"This and that," I said. "I sell things. Or try to. Real estate was the last."

"I don't mean to pry," she said. "But I take it you're not doing anything at the moment?"

"That's right. I'm thinking of going to Arabia with a construction outfit. That's one reason I want to sell the car."

"How soon are you going?"

"Probably sometime next month. Why?"

"Oh, I just wondered." She didn't say anything more

for a minute or two; then she asked, "Are you married?"

"No," I said.

"Did you ever think of making a lot of money?"

"Who hasn't?"

"But did you ever actually think of doing anything about it?"

"Sure. Someday I'm going to invent the incandescent lamp."

"A little soured, Mr. Scarborough? You surely haven't run out of dreams already? At—twenty-eight?"

"Twenty-nine. Look, with a dream and ten cents you can buy a cup of coffee. The only thing I was ever any good at was moving a football from one place to another place, with ten guys helping me. And you need two knees for it. Does this car look like twenty-five hundred bucks to you?"

"A little tough," she murmured. "That's nice."

"Why?"

"I was just thinking again. And I do like the car."

"Then it's a deal?"

She turned her head then and smiled at me. "Maybe," she said. "We might make a deal." She didn't say any more. We drove on down the beach.

When we came back and parked in front of the apartment house she turned off the ignition and started to drop the keys in her purse. I held out my hand for them, saying nothing. Our eyes met, and she shrugged. We got out.

I looked back along the curb, and ahead. "Which is it?" I asked. "The Olds, or that Caddy up there?"

She smiled. "Neither. It's in the garage back in the alley. You notice things, don't you?"

"What's the gag?"

"What makes you think there is one? Maybe I want two cars."

"Do you?"

She looked me right in the face. "No," she said.

I was burning. "What's the idea of wasting my time?"

"Maybe I wasn't."

"No?"

"That's up to you. I said we might make a deal. Remember?"

She went up the stairs and I followed her, remembering the long, relaxed smoothness of her on that towel. She put her purse on the table and tilted the Venetian blinds a little against the light. It was cooler in the apartment and almost dim after the glare in the street. When she turned back I was standing in front of her. I pulled her to me and kissed her, hard, with my hands digging into her back. But she wasn't wasting my time then. I was.

It was all nothing. She rolled with it like a passed-out drunk and didn't even close her eyes. They just watched me coolly. She broke it up with her elbows without seeming to move them, the way they can, and said, "That wasn't quite the deal I had in mind."

"What's wrong with it?" I said.

"Nothing, I suppose, under the right circumstances. But I asked you up here to talk business. Why don't you sit down? You'd probably be more comfortable."

I was still angry, but there was no percentage in knocking myself out. I sat down. She went into the kitchen and came back in a minute with two drinks.

She sat down in a big chair on the other side of the coffee table and crossed her legs. She put a cigarette in her mouth and waited for me to leap up and hold the lighter for her.

The hell with her.

She shrugged and reached for the lighter on the coffee table.

"What is it?" I asked.

She stared thoughtfully at me. "I've been trying to size you up."

"Why?"

"I'm coming to that. I think I can see you now. A little tough—and, what's more to the point, a little cynical, as anybody would be who was a hero at eighteen and a has-been at twenty-five. You sold things for a while, but you sold less and less as time went by and the customers had a little trouble remembering who Lee Scarborough was. You can stop me any time you don't agree with this."

"Go on," I said.

"There was another thing I kept trying to remember. I've got it now. You got in trouble your last year in college and were almost kicked out and nearly went to jail."

"So I smashed up a car," I said.

"It was somebody else's car. And the woman who was smashed up along with it was somebody else's wife. She was in the hospital a long time."

"She got over it," I said. "Without any scars."

"Yes. I guess you would know that."

"All right. Look. There's a type of babe who chases

football players. What're we supposed to do? Scream for help? Or wear chastity girdles?"

She smiled. "You don't have to defend yourself. I'm not accusing you of anything. I'm just trying to see how you fit in the picture. And I think you'll do, on all counts. I want to make you a proposition."

"I hope you have better luck than I did."

"You take women pretty casually, don't you?" she said.

"There's another way?"

"Never mind. But do you want to hear what I asked you up here for?"

"Shoot."

"Remember, I asked you how you'd like to make a lot of money? Well, I think I know where there is a lot of it, for anybody with nerve enough to pick it up."

"Wait a minute," I said. "How do you mean, pick it up? Steal it?"

She shook her head. "No. It's already been stolen. Maybe twice."

I put down my cigarette. She was watching me closely.

"Just how much money?" I asked.

"A hundred and twenty thousand dollars," she said.

Chapter Two

It was very quiet in the room. I whistled softly.

She was still watching me. "How does it sound?"

"I don't know," I said. "I haven't heard anything about it yet."

"All right," she said. "I have to take a chance on somebody if I'm ever going to do anything about it, because I can't do it alone—and I think you're the one. It'll take nerve and intelligence, and it has to be somebody without a criminal record, so the police won't have their eyes on him afterward."

"O.K., O.K.," I said. I knew what she meant. Somebody who wasn't a criminal but who might let a little rub off on him if the price was right. It was a lot of money, but I wanted to hear about it first.

She studied me with speculation in her eyes. "There's a reward for the return of it."

She was sharp. I could see the beauty of that. She was showing me how to do it. You thought about the reward, first; when you got used to that you could let your ideas grow a little. You didn't have to jump in cold. You waded in.

"Whose money is it?" I asked. "And where is it?"

"It's just a long guess," she said. "I didn't say I knew where it was. I said I *think* I know. You add up a lot of things to get to it."

"Such as?"

She took a sip of the drink and looked at me across the top of the glass. "Did you ever hear of a man named J. N. Butler?"

"I don't think so. Who is he?"

"Just a minute."

She got up and went into the bedroom. When she came back she handed me two newspaper clippings. I looked at the first one. It was datelined here in Sanport, June eighth. That was two months ago.

SEARCH WIDENS FOR
MISSING BANK OFFICIAL

J. N. Butler, vice-president of the First National Bank of Mount Temple, was the object of a rapidly expanding manhunt today as announcement was made of discovery of a shortage in the bank's funds estimated at $120,000.

I looked up at her. She smiled. I read on.

Butler, prominent in social and civic activities of the town for over twenty years, has been missing since Saturday, at which time, according to Mrs. Butler, he announced his intention of going to Louisiana for a weekend fishing trip. He did not return Sunday night, as scheduled, but it was not until the bank opened for business this morning that the shortage was discovered.

I read the second one. It was dated three days later, and was a rehash of the previous story, except that the lead paragraph said Butler's car had been found aban-

doned in Sanport and that police were now looking for
him all over the nation.

I handed them back. "That was two months ago," I
said. "What's the pitch? Have they found him?"

"No," she said. "And I don't think they will."

"What do you mean?"

"I don't think he ever left his house in Mount
Temple. Not alive, anyway."

I put the drink down very slowly and watched her
face. You didn't have to be a genius to see she knew
something about it the police didn't.

"Why?" I asked.

"Interested?"

"I might be. Enough to listen, anyway."

"All right," she said. "It's like this: I'm a nurse. And
for about eight months I was on a job in Mount
Temple, taking care of a woman who'd suffered a
stroke and was partially paralyzed. Her house was out
in the edge of town, across the street from a big place,
an enormous old house taking up a whole city block.
J. N. Butler's place." She stopped.

"All right," I said. "Keep going."

"Well, his car, the one they found abandoned
here—I saw it leave there that Saturday. Only it wasn't
Saturday afternoon, the way she said; it was Saturday
night. And he wasn't driving it. She was."

"His wife?"

"His wife."

"Hold it," I said. "You say it was night. How do you
know who was driving?"

"I was out on the front lawn, smoking a cigarette
before going to bed. Just as the Butler car came out of

their drive onto the street, another car went by and caught it in the headlights. It was Mrs. Butler, all right. Alone."

"But," I said, "maybe she was just going to town or something. That doesn't prove he didn't leave in the car later."

She shook her head. "Mrs. Butler never drove his car. She had her own. He didn't abandon that car in Sanport. She did. I'd swear it."

"But why?"

"Don't you see the possibilities?" she said impatiently. "He almost has to be dead. There's no other answer. They'd have found him long ago if he were alive. He was a big, good-looking man, the black-Irish type, easy to see and hard to hide. He was six-three and weighed around two-thirty. You think they couldn't find him? And another thing. When they run like that, ninety-nine times out of a hundred there's another woman in it. Suppose Mrs. Butler found out about it, before he got away? He was going to have the money and the other woman, while she held still for the disgrace. What would she do? Help him pack his bag, to be sure he had plenty of handkerchiefs?"

"I don't know," I said. "What about her?"

She shrugged and gestured with the cigarette. "Who knows who's capable of murder? Maybe anybody is, under the right pressure. But I can tell you a little about her. This is probably an odd thing to say, but she's one of the most beautiful women I've ever seen. Brunette, with a magnolia complexion and big, smoky-looking eyes. And a bitch right out of the book.

Old-family sort of thing; the house is really hers. She also drinks like a fish."

"You didn't miss much while you were up there."

"You mean the drinking? It was one of those hushed-up secrets everybody knows."

"Then," I said, "your idea is she killed Butler? And that the money's still there in the house?"

"Right."

"Didn't the police shake it down?"

"After a fashion. But why would they make much of a search, when he'd obviously got away to Sanport and then disappeared?"

"I see what you mean," I said. "But there's another angle. You say he was a big guy. If she killed him, how did she dispose of his body? She couldn't very well call the piano movers."

She shook her head. "That I don't know. I haven't been able to figure it. But maybe she had a boyfriend. She still had to get back from Sanport, too, after she ditched the car. And, naturally, she couldn't come on the bus. Somebody'd remember it. A boyfriend fits."

"I can see Mrs. Butler rates, in your book," I said. "So far, she's only a lush, a murderer, and a tramp. What'd she do? Dig up your flower beds?"

"Opinions are beside the point. This is for money. What we're trying to get at is facts."

"And all we've got is a string of guesses. Anyway, what's your idea?"

"That we search the house. Tear it apart, if necessary, until we find the money, or some evidence as to what became of Butler, or something."

"With her in it? Think again."

"No," she said. "That's why it takes two of us. She's here in town now, attending a meeting of some historical society. I'll hunt her up, get her plastered, and keep her that way. For days, if necessary. You'll have time to dismantle the house and put it back together before she sobers up enough to go home."

"What you're really looking for," I said, "is a patsy. If something goes wrong, you're all right, but I'm a dead duck."

"Don't be silly. The house is in the middle of an estate that'd cover a city block, with big hedges and trees around it. There's one servant, who goes home as soon as she's out of sight. You could take an orchestra with you, and nobody'd ever know you were in there. The police may check the place once a night when nobody's home, but you don't have to tear off a door and leave it lying on the lawn for them, just to get in. The drapes and curtains will all be drawn. There'll be food in the kitchen. You could set up housekeeping. How about it?"

"It sounds safe enough, for the price," I said. I got up and walked across the room. "But I still don't see it. All that stuff about her leaving there in the car doesn't prove anything. Hell, maybe she was in it with him, and was just covering for him by ditching the car while he got out of town some other way."

She shook her head. "No. I tell you he's dead. And she killed him. That money's still there."

"I can't see why you're so sure," I said.

"Then you don't believe I'm right?" she said. "You don't want to tackle it?"

I thought about the money. A hundred and twenty

thousand. You couldn't get hold of it all at once. It was
too big. It had to grow on you.

I let it grow.

But, hell. She was crazy. In that whole story of hers
there wasn't one shred of evidence that Butler hadn't
got away with it. A lot of good guesses, maybe, but no
concrete evidence. And if you were going to take a
chance and start breaking laws like that, you had to
have something more definite than a guess to lead you
on. I couldn't see it.

"Well?" she asked. "How about it?"

"The whole thing's a pipe dream," I said.

"You're passing up a fortune."

I shrugged. "I doubt it."

I tried another pass but she wasn't having any, so I
said, "See you around," and shoved off. I punched
Winlock's buzzer on the way downstairs, but he still
wasn't home.

I got in the car and looked at my watch. It was after
five. The whole afternoon was shot. I went home,
picking up my mail on the way in through the lobby, and
wondering how much longer I'd be able to pay the rent.
It was more apartment than I needed, or could afford,
in a new building with a lot of glass brick and thick car-
pets, over on Davy Avenue. I'd moved into it when I
first went with Wagner Realty and was going to make a
thousand a month selling houses in a subdivision. That
was in May, and when they dusted off the old wheeze
about a reduction in force three days ago, on the first of
August, I was still working on the first month's thousand. Maybe the demand for ten-thousand-dollar apple
crates was falling off, or I was no salesman.

I sat down in the living room and looked at the mail. It was all bills except one letter on orchid stationery. I tried to recall who the girl was, but finally gave up and looked at the bills. The tailor called my attention very tactfully to $225 that I had apparently overlooked last month and the month before. There was another note due on the car. I shuffled through the others: two department stores, the utilities, and the kennel that boarded Moxie, the English setter. I checked my bank balance. I had $170.

I went out in the kitchen and tried to convince myself I ought to have a drink. After looking at the bottle, I shoved it back on the shelf, losing interest in it. I never drank much, and I still had the sour taste of those others in my mouth. I thought of her. I thought of her on that towel. The hell with all dizzy women, anyway. The whole afternoon shot, I hadn't sold the car, and I didn't even get the consolation prize. No sale, no loving, I thought disgustedly, saying it so it rhymed. The whole afternoon shot to hell. It would probably have been pretty good stuff, too.

That bank balance couldn't have been right. A hundred and seventy— I checked it again.

It was right.

I thought of Saudi Arabia, of 120-degree heat and sand and the wind blowing for two years, and wondered if I could take it. But before long it wasn't going to be a question of whether I could stand it or not. I had to do something. I made less money every year.

You got your brains beat out for four years for seventy dollars a month plus your tuition and having some old grad pounding you on the back to get into the pictures after you'd scored from eight yards out in the last three seconds of play in the Homecoming game, and five years later the son-of-a-bitch couldn't remember your name when you tried to send it in past the arctic blonde in the outer office.

I put a cigarette in my mouth, reaching for the lighter, and then let it hang there, forgotten. Half of $120,000...

I shrugged irritably. Was I going to start that again? Maybe I was going back to believing in Santa Claus. Diana James was just a victim of wishful thinking, trying to build something out of a half-baked theory. But still, she didn't quite strike me as that kind of featherhead.

Why was she so sure? That was the thing I couldn't see. It didn't match up with the flimsy evidence of her story. And why hadn't the police found him? Something rang there, too. They should have picked him up long ago, a big, good-looking guy like that with no place to hide. I didn't know much about police work, but it seemed to me embezzlers should be the easiest of all lamsters to collar; the people who were looking for them knew too much about them. They'd have pictures of him, a complete knowledge of all his habits, everything. His car had been abandoned here in a city of four hundred thousand, and then he had vanished like a wisp of smoke. It could happen. But the odds were very long against it.

The whole thing was just crazy enough to make you wonder.

And the amount was too big to get out of your mind.

I cursed, and went back down to the car. I drove

over to the library and asked for the back files of the
Sanport *Citizen*. Beginning with the first of August, I
worked back toward June. In the fourth paper I found
another story on it. It was datelined Sanport, July 27.

NO SOLUTION IN
BUTLER DISAPPEARANCE

*After nearly two months of a nationwide manhunt,
police announced today there has been no new
light whatever thrown on the possible whereabouts
of the Mount Temple bank official who allegedly
absconded with $120,000 of the bank's funds. Since
the discovery on June 11 of Butler's car, abandoned
on a local street near the beach…*

Well, there wasn't anything new in that, except the
fact that they definitely hadn't found him.

I sat suddenly upright in the chair. The thing that
had been bothering me all the time was just beyond
my reach. I looked back at the story: "…Butler's car,
abandoned on a local street near the beach…" That
was it.

That second clipping she had shown me, the one
carrying the story about the car, had given the name of
the street. It hadn't sunk in at the time, but it had been
bothering my subconscious ever since. I grabbed
another bundle of the papers and began flipping hurriedly through them. June 14, June 13, June 11—it
should be in this one. I shot my glance up column and
down, across the front page. Here it was.

"The late-model automobile of the missing man was

discovered early today abandoned near the beach in
the 200 block of Duval Boulevard."

I wondered why I had let it slide off the first time
I'd read it. It was given right in Winlock's ad, the thing
that had taken me out there in the first place. The
address of that apartment house was 220 Duval
Boulevard.

I was beginning to have an idea why she was so sure
Butler was dead.

Chapter Three

She came down and let me in when I rang the buzzer. Neither of us said anything until we were back up in the living room. She sat down in the same place she'd been before, across the coffee table, and smiled at me, the eyes cool and a little amused.

"I wondered if you'd be back," she said. "And how soon."

"Why didn't you tell me?"

She lit a cigarette and looked thoughtfully at the smoke. "Let's put it this way: If you didn't have sense enough to see it, you wouldn't be smart enough to be of any help. This is no child's game, you know. And it could be dangerous as hell."

"There's one thing I'm still not too sure of," I said. "And that's why you're so certain *she's* the one that killed him and left his car in front of your apartment. Wasn't there anybody else who could have known he was going to run off with you?"

"It's not likely. And nobody but that vindictive bitch would have gone to that much trouble and risk of exposure just for the pleasure of letting me know. I mean, leaving the car right out front here. She would do that."

"How about telling me the whole thing?" I said.

"Suppose you tell me something first," she said coolly. "Do you want in this, or don't you?"

"What do you think? I came back, didn't I?"

"Not worried about breaking the law?"

"Let's put it this way: Whoever's got that money is outside the law himself, or herself. So he or she can't yell cop. And as far as conscience is concerned, you can buy a lot of sleeping pills with sixty thousand dollars."

She raised her eyebrows. "Who said anything about sixty thousand? I'm offering you a third."

"And you know what you can do with your third. It's half or nothing."

"You've got a nerve—"

"What do you mean, nerve? I'm the one that has to go up there and stick his head in the lion's mouth and search the place. You don't take any risk."

"All right, all right," she said. "Relax. I just thought I'd try. A half it is."

"That's better. Now, tell me about it."

"All right," she said. "You know now why I'm so certain he's dead. He has to be, or he'd have shown up here. Butler was no fool. He knew he didn't have a chance unless he had a place to hide. So he and I worked it out. I got this apartment several months before he pulled it off. When he took the money and made the break he was to come here, hide in this apartment without even going out on the street for at least two months, until some of the uproar had died down and we had changed his appearance as much as possible. Then we were going to get away to the West Coast in a car and trailer, with Butler riding in the trailer. He'd turn up in San Francisco with a whole new identity. It was a fine idea, of course, except that he never did show up here. His car did, but somebody else drove it."

"That's right."

"So you believe me now?" she said.

"Yes. Certainly. That was the thing that made the difference. The other story didn't make any sense. As soon as it soaked into my head that you were the woman he was running off with— And, of course, if he didn't show up here, it was because he couldn't."

"So the money's still right there in the house in Mount Temple," she said.

"That I'm not so sure of. Anybody might have killed him, for that much."

"No. Nobody else could have known about it. But she did. The last time I saw him he was afraid she'd put detectives on our trail."

"How long have you known them?" I asked. "Were you actually a nurse there in Mount Temple?"

"Yes. But that was last fall and winter. I'd been back here four months when he actually pulled it off."

"He was pretty gone on you?"

"Maybe. In a way," she said.

"You after him? Or the money?"

"Let's say both. We believed in taking what we needed, and what we needed was each other. What do you want? Tristan and Isolde?"

"And now that he's dead, you'll settle for the money?" Then I changed it. "For half the money."

"That's right. What should I do? Throw myself off a cliff?"

"We'll get along," I said.

She crushed the cigarette out with a savage slash at

the ashtray. "There's another thing, too. She's not going to get away with it. The drunken bitch."

Well, I thought, I'll be a sad...

"Get this through your head," I said. "Once and for all. This is a business proposition, or I'm out, as of now. There'll be no wild-haired babes blowing their tops and killing each other in anything I'm mixed up in. I thought you were tough."

She glared at me. "I am," she said. "What I mean is she's not going to get away with the money."

"That's better. Just keep it in mind."

"Mount Temple's about two hundred miles away," I said. "I can drive it in four hours."

She shook her head. "You'll have to go on the bus."

"What do you mean, go on the bus?"

"Look. You'll be in that house two days. Maybe three. Where are you going to leave your car? In the drive?"

"I'll park it somewhere else in town."

"No. In that length of time somebody might notice it. The police might impound it. A hundred things could happen."

I could see she was right. A car with out-of-town tags sitting around that long might attract attention. But the bus idea wasn't much better.

"I'm supposed to get in there and out without being seen by anybody who could identify me afterward. The bus is no good."

She nodded. "That's right, too. We can't be too careful about that. I think the best thing is for me to drive you up there."

"Listen," I said. "Here's the way we work it. You

drive me up there, drop me off in back somewhere
where there's no street light, then come back and keep
an eye on Mrs. Butler. This is Tuesday night. If the
house is as big as you say it is, I'll want two full days. So
at exactly two o'clock Friday morning you ease by in
back of the place again and I'll be out there waiting for
you. We'll either have the money, or we'll know it's not
there."

"Right." She leaned back in her chair and stared at
me with her eyes a little cool and hard. "And just in
case you haven't thought of it yet," she said, "don't get
any brilliant ideas about running out with all of it if
you find it, just because I'm not there. You know how
far you'd get as soon as the police received an anonymous phone call."

She had it figured from every angle. "You're sweet,"
I said. "Who'd run off from you?"

"For that much money, you would. But don't try it."

"Right," I said. "And while we're on the subject,
don't try to double-cross me, either."

I held my wrist under the dash lights and looked at the
watch. It was three-ten.

We had left Sanport at midnight, after I had put my
own car in a storage garage and bought a few things I'd
need. I checked them off in my mind: flashlight with
spare batteries, small screwdriver, Scotch tape, half a
dozen packs of cigarettes. It was all there.

She was driving fast, around sixty most of the time.
There was very little traffic, and the towns along the
highway were asleep. We came into one now, and she
slowed to thirty-five as we went through.

"It's the next one," she said. "About thirty miles."

"You won't get back until after daylight."

"It doesn't matter. Nobody knows me there. And Mrs. Butler probably won't be up before noon."

"The police may be tailing her. Just on the chance she might be meeting Butler."

"I know." She punched the cigarette lighter and said, "Give me a cigarette, Lee. But what if they are? They don't know anything."

When the lighter popped out, I lit the cigarette and handed it to her. We were running through a long river bottom now, with dark walls of trees on both sides. I looked at her. She had put on a long, pleated white skirt and maroon blouse. She was a smooth job, with the glow of the dash highlighting the rounded contours of her face and shining in the big dark eyes.

I lit one for myself. "There's one thing I still don't like," I said. "There may be a lot of that money in negotiable securities instead of cash. I mean, he was a banker and he'd know how to convert 'em without getting tripped up, but we wouldn't."

"No," she said. "He was going to get it all in cash. He was going to pick the time when he could get it that way."

"Good," I said. "God, that's a wad of dough."

"Isn't it?"

"It would be a pretty good-sized briefcaseful, figuring a lot of it would be in tens and twenties. What kind of hiding place would you look for, if you had to stash it around a house?"

"It's an old house," she said. "A very old house, and a big one. The only thing to do is start at the attic and work down, taking it a room at a time. Look for places that appear to have been repapered recently or where there's been some repair work, like around window sills and doorframes. Trap doors above clothes closets, in the floors or walls. And remember, she's plenty smart. She's just as likely to wrap it in old paper and throw it in a trunk or a barrel of rubbish. Take your time, and tear the house apart if you have to. She's in no position to call the police."

"We hope," I said.

"We know."

"All right," I said. "But I still don't want her to catch me in there just to see if we're right. So I've been trying to figure out some way you can tip me off if she gets away from you and you think she's on her way home. I think I've got it. Call the house, long-distance, and—"

"But, my God, you couldn't answer the phone if it rang. There's no way you could tell who it was."

"Wait till I finish," I said. "Of course I won't answer until I'm sure it's you. Here's the way. Call right on the hour. I won't answer, so put the call in again at a quarter past, as near as you can make it. I won't answer then, either, because it still might be a coincidence. But repeat it again, as near half past as you can, and I'll pick it up. Just ask if Mrs. Butler is better. I'll say yes, and hang up and get the hell out of there."

I thought about it again. "No. Wait. There's no reason I should have to answer at all. Those three calls, fifteen minutes apart, will be the signal. When I hear the third one, I scram."

"That's good," she said, nodding. "You know how to

use your head. It's funny, but in a lot of ways you're just like Butler."

"Not too much, I hope."

"Why?" she asked.

"He's dead. Remember?"

She fell silent. We came up out of the river country and ran through rolling hills with dark farmhouses here and there along the road. In a few minutes she said, "We're almost there. It's on the left as we go into town."

I looked, but it was too dark to see much. All I got was the shadowy impression of a house set far back from the street among the darker gloom of big trees. There was no light anywhere. We made a gentle turn to the right and then were on the street going into town, with houses and lawns on both sides. About three blocks up a street light hung out over an inter-section. She turned left before we got to it, went a block down a side street, and turned left again.

"When I stop," she said, "we'll be right behind the place. There's a big oleander hedge and a woven-wire fence, but the gate probably won't be locked. Or if it is, you can climb over or go around in front. Good luck."

"Check," I said. "Friday morning at two o'clock. Right here."

She was slowing. The car came to a standstill for not more than two seconds. I slid out and eased the door shut. Her hand lifted and the car slid away. I was on my own.

The red taillights of the car swung left and disap-peared. I stepped off the street and stood for a moment while my eyes adjusted themselves to the darkness. There was no moon, and the night was hot and still. Somewhere across town a dog barked. I could see the dark line of the oleanders in front of me now, and started walking toward them, putting out my hand. I touched the fence, and walked parallel to it, looking for the gate and a break in the hedge.

I'd forgotten to look at my watch again before I got out of the car, but I should have nearly two hours until daybreak. It was plenty of time to find a way into the house.

I went twenty steps along the fence. Thirty. There had to be a gate somewhere. She'd said there was. I came to a corner. There was no opening. I had gone the wrong way. I turned and went back, touching the fence with my hands. It was six feet high, with steel posts. The oleanders were on the inside, a solid wall of them nearly fifteen feet high.

I found the gate. It rattled a little when I put my hand on it. I felt along one side for the latch and located it. Apparently there was no chain or padlock. I eased it open. A dry hinge squeaked in the silence. I stopped, then pulled it open very slowly.

I could see the dark bulk of the house looming ahead of me now across the expanse of rear lawn. It was enormous, two stories and an attic, probably, with high gables running off into the big overhanging trees at each end. Off to the right was a smaller pile of blackness, which I took to be the garage.

I stepped inside, through the break in the hedge, and studied the blank windows carefully for any sliver of light at all. There was none. The whole place was as

dark and deserted and silent as if it had been vacant
for twenty years.

I eased across the grass toward the back porch.
Then, suddenly, I thought of something we had over-
looked. We hadn't thought of the grounds themselves.
There were probably two acres of trees, flower beds,
shrubs, and lawns around the place. If the money—or
even Butler's body—had been buried out here somewhere, it would take a gang of men with a bulldozer a
week to search it all. We'd been stupid.

But what could we do about it, if we had thought of
it? Our only hope was that the stuff was in the house.
If I didn't find it there, we were whipped. The only
thing to do was go on.

I came to the corner of the porch and went around
it to the rear of the house itself. In the darkness I
could just make out the forms of two windows set close
to the ground and partially screened by shrubs. They
were just what I had been hoping to find—basement
windows.

I slipped up to the first and took out the small flashlight. Standing close to shield it with my body, I shot
the tiny beam inside. The screen and the window were
both dirty, but I could see the latch where the top and
bottom sashes met. It was closed. I moved to the other
window. It was latched too.

Probably they all are, I thought. I stood back a little
and sized them up. This one was better screened
behind the shrubs. Getting down on my knees, I
turned the light on again and shot it in on the hook at
the bottom of the screen. I took out the screwdriver,
pushed the blade in through the wire, and pried at the

hook. It slid out, and the screen was free. I swung the bottom of it outward against the shrub and got in behind it.

Taking the Scotch tape out of my pocket, I began peeling it off and plastering strips of it across the glass of the upper sash, crisscrossing it in all directions. Then I reversed the screwdriver and rapped smartly with the handle right in front of the latch. The glass cracked, but the tape kept it from falling. I slid the screwdriver blade through against the latch, and pushed. It slid open.

I raised the bottom sash, swung the beam of light down inside, and dropped in. Pulling the screen back in place, I hooked it and closed the window. I took a quick look around the basement. This must be only part of it. It was a big room with a furnace in the center. Against the opposite wall was a coal bin, and beside it were some old trunks and a pile of magazines and newspapers. I saw a door, and went through it. This room held a washing machine and a lot of clotheslines.

There was no use trying to search this now. What I had to do first was take a quick look at the whole house and size up the job—and make certain that maid wasn't here. Diana James had said she'd be gone, but it wasn't Diana James that was going to wind up behind the eight ball if she happened to be wrong.

I went back in the first room and started swinging the light around, looking for the stairway. I'd just spotted it, over against the rear wall, when I stopped dead still and cut the light. I held my breath, listening. I could hear my heart beating in the dead, oppressive

silence, and the hair along the back of my neck was
still prickling. The place was making me jumpy.

What I'd thought I heard was music.

Music at four o'clock in the morning in an empty
house? Nuts. I listened for another full minute and
then flicked the light on again. I went up the stairs.
There was a door at the top of them. I opened it softly
and went through. I was in the kitchen.

There was a window over the sink, but the curtains
were drawn. That was something I had to check in all
the rooms, so I could move around freely during the
day. I examined the rest of the room. The door by the
sink must be the one going out onto the back porch.
The one on this side, beyond the stove, apparently
led into the dining room and the front of the house.
This left one more, besides the cellar door I'd just
come through. It was at the end of the kitchen, and it
was closed. I had to see in there. It should be the
maid's room.

I eased over to it, got my hand on the knob, and cut
the light. I turned it slowly, very slowly, and pushed. It
swung open into more of the same impenetrable darkness. I stood perfectly still, listening for the sound of
breathing. It was the maid's room, all right.

The room was full of her, but that didn't mean she
was here now. What I was smelling was the place she
lived in. But I had to know, and know now, before it
was daylight and too late to get out. I flicked the light
on, pointed straight down, my nerves tightened up for
the scream that would split the night. Or the gun blast
that'll blow my stupid head off, I thought, if she's here
and she's got company. I was sweating. I eased the

beam forward. It hit the end of a bed, climbed it. The bed was empty. I breathed again.

I closed the door and walked back through the kitchen. The drapes were drawn in the dining room. The table and sideboards were old, massive, and very dark. One of the sideboards was covered with an ornate old silver service that had probably cost somebody's ancestor a young fortune.

I walked on into the living room and inspected it in the beam of light. No wonder Mrs. Butler's a lush, I thought. Living in a mausoleum like this would make anybody take to the juice. It was an enormous room, furnished the same way the dining room was. The woodwork was all mahogany and walnut, and dark with age. The drapes, which were drawn, looked like wine-colored velvet, and the sofas and chairs were upholstered in maroon plush—the ones that weren't black leather. One whole wall was covered with books.

I stopped the light suddenly, staring at the rows of books. I backed it up a little. Then I brought it ahead, very slowly, watching. It was odd. The volumes of the encyclopedia were all jumbled, in no order at all, and there were other books sandwiched in between them.

I began to have an odd hunch then. I threw the light around over the rest of the room again. Everything else seemed to be in order and in its place. I got down on my hands and knees beside one of the sofas and looked at the dents in the rug where the feet rested. It had been moved recently, all right. But that didn't mean anything. The maid had probably done it, cleaning.

Picking up one end of the sofa, I swung it away

from the wall and looked at the back of it. I saw it then. It was a long slash in the cloth, made by a sharp knife or razor blade. I began snatching up the cushions. They were all slashed on the undersides. So were the ones in the chairs.

For an instant I wanted to throw the flashlight through the window. Then I settled down a little, and squatted on my heels to light a cigarette. Who was it? No, the question was: Had he found what he was looking for? There was a chance he hadn't.

But, if not, why wasn't he still here, looking for it? That was the one you couldn't get around.

Was there a chance it was just the search the police had given the place, two months ago? No. They wouldn't have cut things up that way. And Mrs. Butler or the maid would have put the books back in some sort of order by this time. This had been done recently.

But there was one thing about it. The fact that somebody else had been searching the place proved we were right. Apparently we weren't the only ones who had reason to believe Mrs. Butler had killed her husband before he could get away.

And I was here, wasn't I? And I was going to be here until Friday morning. What did I want to do— quit before I'd even got started? What the hell. Go ahead and search the place. That was what I'd come for. Maybe the other people hadn't found it. I located an ashtray and crushed out the cigarette. The thought of the money was making me itchy again.

I went out through an archway at the end of the living room. There was a short hall here, or entry, with the front door at one end and the stairs at the other. I started up the stairs.

The steps were carpeted, but halfway up one of them creaked under my weight. I stopped, cursing silently; then I shook off the jumpiness. What was I worried about? I had the whole place to myself, didn't I? The maid was gone.

I reached the top. I started to turn, sweeping the flashlight beam ahead of me. Then I froze dead and snapped it off, staring down the hallway. A door was open on one side of it, and I could see a very faint glow of light spilling out into the hall. I put my other foot down silently and eased the awkward position I was in. I wanted to turn and run, but something about the light fascinated me. I remained motionless, hardly breathing.

It was too dim to be an electric light of any kind, and it seemed to flicker. Was it a match? Maybe whoever it was was setting fire to the place. But no, it didn't seem to grow, as a fire would. I waited. It remained the same. Then I knew what it was. It was a candle.

That didn't make any sense. Who'd be wandering around with a candle, with flashlights selling for forty-nine cents? But before I could even start to think about it, I became conscious of something new. It was a sound. It was a faint hissing noise, coming from the room.

Then, at almost the same time I guessed what it was, the music started. It had been the needle riding in the groove, of a phonograph record. The music was turned down very low, and it was something long-hair I didn't recognize.

I knew I should run, but I didn't. I couldn't. I had to look in there. It was only three or four steps down the hall. There was a carpet to muffle the sound of my steps.

I stopped just short of the door. This was the dangerous part of it. Whoever was in there would be able to see me when I looked in if he happened to be facing the door. The music went on very softly, but there was no other sound. I put my face against the doorframe and peered around it.

It was a strange sight. At first there was an odd feeling about it, as if I had wandered into some kind of religious ceremony. Then I began to get it sorted out. It was a bedroom. The candle was burning on the floor in a little silver dish, and beside it was the record player. Phonograph records were scattered around on the rug, and in the middle of them, alongside a low couch, a girl in a long blue robe sat on the floor and swayed gently back and forth as she listened to the music.

I saw her in profile with the candlelight softly touching her face and the cloud of dark hair that swirled about it. She was almost unbelievably beautiful, and she was drunk as a lord.

I remained very still outside the door, thinking coldly of Diana James. Mrs. Butler was like hell in Sanport.

Chapter Four

Had she thrown that curve deliberately, or had it just been a mix-up? She'd lied right at the beginning, because she didn't want to tell me any more about the thing than she had to. Maybe she'd lied again.

But maybe it had just been an accident. Mrs. Butler must have come back from Sanport unexpectedly, without her hearing about it. It made sense that way. We wanted the money. To find it, we had to search the house. So there was nothing she stood to gain by getting me to come up here to try to shake it down with Mrs. Butler in it.

Was there?

I couldn't see anything. But the next time I took anybody's word...I was still burning.

Well, we could kiss off any chance of finding it now. The thing I had to do was get out of there as fast as I could, before daylight. If I waited too long, somebody might spot me leaving. Once I got off the grounds I'd be all right. I could walk into town and hang around until there was a bus leaving for Sanport. And when I got back there I'd break the news to Diana James as to what I thought of her and her information.

I remained standing there, sick with rage at the idea of having to give up. Somehow it seemed I had already come to consider the money as mine, as already found and safe in my pocket, and now that it was snatched away I was wild with a sense of loss, as if somebody had robbed me. Why didn't I lock her in a closet and go on with the search as soon as it was light?

No. That would be too dangerous. Discovery was almost certain. The maid would come back. She might have visitors. I'd be caught. I discarded the idea, but I did not leave.

There was no danger. Not from her. She was too plastered to notice anything, or to do anything about it if she did see me. If I walked in and started talking to her, she'd probably just think I was another form of the jim-jams. I could see the half-empty bottle, and the glass that had fallen over on its side. She wasn't a noisy drunk, or a sloppy one. It was just the opposite. The thing that tipped you off was the exaggerated dignity, and the slow, deliberate way she moved, as if she were made of eggshells.

The record ran out to the end and ground to a stop as the machine shut itself off. It was deadly silent with the music gone. She made no attempt to put on another record. She was still swaying a little, and I could see her lips moving as if she were singing to herself or praying, but no sound came out. Then, very slowly, she turned the upper part of her body a little and collapsed against the low divan beside her. Her face was pressed into the covering, the dark hair aswirl, and one arm stretched out across it.

I started to turn away. It was time to get out of there. Then I stopped suddenly and swung my head around, listening. What I'd heard wasn't repeated. It didn't have to be; I knew what it was. It was that step, the same one that had creaked under me. Somebody was coming up the stairs.

There was another room opening off the hall, but the door was closed. He'd hear me open it. I didn't have all night to make up my mind. I slid inside, leaned over Mrs. Butler, and blew out the candle. I'd already seen the closet door partly open beyond her.

When the blackness closed in I kept the picture of the room in my mind long enough to turn ninety degrees to the right, slip past the end of the divan, and grope for the door of the closet. I touched it, eased it open, and stepped inside. Clothes brushed against my back. They smelled faintly of perfume in the hot, dead air.

There was no sound. But the hallway was carpeted. Whoever it was could be anywhere out there. I waited, keeping an eye to the crack in the door. A beam of light appeared in the doorway of the room and swung around the walls. It hit a mirror and splashed, then swept on. It dipped, catching the pile of phonograph records and the whisky bottle, and came to rest at last on the sprawled figure of the girl. It remained fixed, like a big eye, while whoever was holding the flashlight walked on into the room. It was so still I tried to quiet the sound of my breathing.

He was squatting down now, and seemed to be changing hands with the light. Then I saw why. Just for a second the gun passed through the beam, steadying up against her temple. The cold-blooded brutality of it made me come out of the closet without even stopping to think.

I was driving, the way they teach you to get up a head

of steam in the first three strides. But I forgot the end of the divan. My legs hit it, and I went the rest of the way in by air. He was under me and trying to turn when I sifted down on him, and from then on it was confused, and rough. When nothing crunched, I knew he was no fly-weight himself, and as we rolled across and demolished the record player I could feel the tremendous surge of power in the arm about my neck. The light had gone out when it hit the floor, so we were in absolute darkness, and I didn't know what had become of the gun.

The arm was pulling my head off. I broke it up by getting a knee into his belly and starting to move it down to where he didn't like it. He scuttled away from it and landed a big fist on the side of my face. It rocked me. I could feel it going all the way down to my toes and back up again like a shock wave. I shook my head, trying to clear it, and swung blindly in the dark. I missed. I heard him scrambling away. He was on his feet. He crashed into the doorframe, and then he was gone down the hall.

I sat up dizzily and dug my own flashlight out of my pocket. He might or might not leave the house, and it made a lot of difference now who had the gun. I held the light out from my side and snapped it on, shooting it around the floor. The gun was lying in a hash of broken phonograph records, and his light was on the floor the other side of what was left of the player. I picked up the gun, checked the safety, and put it in my pocket, conscious of the heavy way I was breathing. It had been short, but it had been rugged.

I squatted on the floor to get my breath. Whoever he was, he was probably gone by now. I had the gun, so it wasn't likely he'd tackle me again. I could leave. Provided, of course, I didn't run into half a dozen more on the way out.

I thought of Diana James. She was cute. She just needed somebody to search this old vacant house. There was nothing to it. And if the first sucker she sent got killed, she could always find more. Well, she was going to get a sucker's full report when I got back to Sanport.

I stood up. I'd better get started. Flicking on the light again, I looked down at the girl. Her shoulders had fallen off the divan and she was lying on the floor beside it with her head on an outstretched arm. She was going to have an awful headache in the morning, I thought, when she tried to figure out how she could have wrecked the room this way. It would be a rough way to wake up.

I got it then. If I left, she wasn't going to wake up.

That guy had come here to kill her. He'd wait around until he saw me shove off, then he'd finish the job I had interrupted. He didn't need the gun. She was asleep; he could kill her with anything. He was good when they were asleep. You could see that.

Well, what was I supposed to do? So I didn't have the stomach to sit there and see her butchered in cold blood; so now I was the protector of the poor? The hell with it. If I hung around here until she sobered up, she'd probably have me arrested for burglary. And I could just tell the cops how it happened, couldn't I? They didn't get many laughs in their work. Housebreaker saves woman's life. Hey, Joe, come listen to this one.

Then a very chilling thought caught up with me. Suppose they found her in here murdered, tomorrow or the next day? Maybe nobody on earth knew that other guy was here. But there was one person who knew damn well I'd been here, because she'd brought me here. And if she ever leaked, I'd be in the worst jam I'd ever heard of.

I had to do something. Time was running out. I squatted there in the dark, thinking swiftly. I began to see it then. It was the answer to everything.

Here was where I went in business for myself.

All I'd accomplished in this thing so far was to get shoved around. I'd been played for a sucker by a smooth operator who'd told me about 10 percent of the whole story, but now the program was going to change.

We were all looking for that money. And the only person that really knew whether or not it was in this house was Mrs. Butler. She was the key to the whole thing. I didn't believe now that it was here, but she knew where it was, or where it was last seen. So what I wanted was Mrs. Butler. If I left her here she'd be killed, but if I took her with me I'd have the exact thing I needed: information.

And I knew just where to take her where we wouldn't be interrupted. I could sober her up, and maybe if I kept asking the right questions long enough, I might find out a little about this. Of course, if she *didn't* have anything to do with killing Butler, I was laying myself wide open to arrest for kidnapping, but I could see the way out of that. I tried to visualize the road map in my mind. It couldn't be much over fifty miles....

It collapsed on me then. Take her? How? I didn't have my car. Load her on my shoulder like a sack of oats, and walk through town with her? I cursed under my breath. I was right back where I'd started. But wait. She had a car, didn't she? She must have come back from Sanport in it.

I'd have to leave her while I went out to the garage to look. But that joker probably wouldn't try to ease back until he was sure I was gone. I went out and down the stairs, hurrying. I unlocked the kitchen door leading onto the back porch, cut the light, and went out. It was a few seconds before I could see anything in the dark. It'd be a nice time, I thought, for the gruesome bastard to try to clobber me with an ax.

When I could make out the squat shadow of the garage off beyond the corner of the house, I groped my way over to it. The big overhead door was locked. I went around to the side. There was a small door there. I tried the knob. It was unlocked. I went in and closed it. When I switched on the flashlight I was standing beside a '53 Cadillac. I poked the beam in on the dash. The keys weren't in it. All I had to do now was find them. In a house of about twenty rooms. I looked at my watch. It was four-twenty. Maybe I couldn't make it now, even if I already had the keys.

I'd never pretended to be able to think like a woman, but I knew a little about drunks. It paid off. I covered the area between the front door, where she would come in, and the kitchen, where the bottle would be, and I found the purse on a table by the dining room door. Her key case was in it.

I left it where it was and went back upstairs. I had

picked her up and started out of the room when I
thought of something else. Putting her down on the
divan, I flashed the light around on the floor, looking
for the bottle. It had been knocked over during the
fight, but it was corked and none of it had spilled. It
was a fifth, a little over half full. I shoved it in my
coat pocket and picked her up again. She was still
out like a hung jury, and I knew she would be for
hours. As I went out through the kitchen I grabbed
up the purse.

I put her on the back seat of the car and switched
on the flashlight long enough to take a look at the keys.
I sorted out a couple that looked promising, cut the
light, and went back outside, feeling for the lock of the
overhead door. The first key did the trick. I boosted
the door up slowly and got back in the car. Picking
out the ignition key by feel, I started the Caddy and
backed it out onto the driveway. The drive was white
gravel and I could see it all right, all the way out to
the big gates in front. I swung out onto the street and
felt my way very slowly for another hundred yards.
Then I switched on the headlights and goosed the two
hundred horses.

Housebreaking, I thought. Auto theft. Abduction.
What was next? Blackmail? Extortion? But I had it all
figured now, I was still within jumping distance of
solid ground in every direction, and I wasn't in much
danger if I played it right. Somebody was going to
come home first in that $120,000 sweepstakes, and as
of now I looked like the favorite.

We were headed south, on the highway we'd come
in on. I rolled it up to seventy and tried to remember

where the turnoff was. It should be somewhere around ten miles beyond that next town. I'd just have to watch for it, because I wasn't too sure, approaching it from this direction. I'd been there plenty of times, but had always come up from the south.

The headlights of a car behind us hit the rear-view mirror. I watched them for a minute. It probably didn't mean anything; there were always a few cars on the road, even at four-thirty in the morning. They continued to hang in about the same place, not gaining or falling back.

Maybe the joker'd had a car there and was trying to find out where we went. We were dipping down toward that long piece of tangent across the river bottom now. We'll see, chum, I thought. I flipped the lights on high beam and gunned it.

I flattened it out at ninety-five and the swamp and timber flashed past and disappeared behind us in the night with just the long sucking sound of the wind. I couldn't watch him now because I couldn't take my eyes off the road, but when we came out onto the winding grade at the other end I eased it down and looked. He'd dropped back, but only a little.

That was dumb, I thought. Suppose it was a highway cop pacing us? But it wasn't; he made no attempt to haul us down. He was just hanging there. I was still worrying about the turnoff. There was still only a slight chance he was following us, but I didn't want him to see where we left the highway.

We blasted through the little town and I began counting off the miles on the speedometer. The road was winding now, and he was out of sight most of the time. But I had to ease it, looking for the place. We'd come nine miles. Ten. Eleven. Had I passed it?

Then we careened around a long curve and I saw the huddled dark buildings of the country store and filling station. I rode it down and made the turn, throwing gravel as we left the pavement. The county road ran straight ahead through dark walls of pine. I stepped on the brakes again and snapped off the lights as we slid to a stop. In a minute I saw his lights as he went rocketing past on the highway. I sighed with relief. It was probably some guy named Joe, in the wholesale grocery business.

I cut the lights back on and before we started up I looked at my watch. It was a little after five. We still had about twenty miles to go, and I wanted to get past the last houses on the way before daybreak. We could make it if we kept moving.

Two miles ahead I turned right and followed a county road going south through scrub pine. I knew the way all right now. I'd been up here a dozen times or more with Bill Livingston, and sometimes alone, or with a girl. It was his camp I was headed for.

We'd been friends in college. His family had left him a lot of money and five or ten thousand acres of land back in here, including the lake where the camp was and a bunch of sloughs and river bottom. He was in Europe for the summer, but I knew where he left the key to the place.

I slowed, watching for the wire gate on the left side of the road. We came to it in a few minutes, went through, and I closed it again. It was eight miles of rough private road now, up over a series of sand hills and then dropping down toward the lake. The last time I'd been in they were cutting timber back in here somewhere and logging trucks were using the first three or four miles of the road. I could see the tread marks of their big tires in the ruts now. There was no way to tell whether any other cars had been in or not.

I pushed it hard. In about ten minutes we came to the fork where the logging trucks swung off to the right. I went left. As soon as we were around the next bend I stopped and got out and looked at the ruts in the headlights. There hadn't been a car through since the last time it had rained, probably weeks ago. We had it all to ourselves.

Dawn was breaking as we came down the last grade. I caught glimpses of the arm of the lake ahead, dark and oily smooth, like blued steel, with patches of mist rising here and there in the timber. It was intensely quiet, and beautiful. For a minute I wished I were only going fishing. Then I brushed it off.

We went through the meadow and crossed a wooden culvert at the edge of the trees along the lake shore. I stopped and got out. The key was hanging on a nail just inside one end of the culvert.

The cabin faced the meadow rather than the lake. It was large for a fishing or duck-hunting camp, more like a deserted old farmhouse backed up among the big trees at the lake's edge. It was still half dark back in here, and I left the lights on as I stopped by the overhang of the front porch.

The lock grated in the early-morning hush. I pushed the door open and went in. Striking a match,

I located one of the kerosene lamps and lit it. This was the main room, with a wood-burning kitchen stove and some cupboards in the rear and a cot and some chairs and a table up front. The door on the right led into a storeroom that was cluttered with a hundred or so old beat-up duck decoys, parts of outboard motors, some oars, and a welter of fishing tackle.

The other one, on the left, was closed. I pushed it open and carried the lamp in. It was the bedroom. It held two built-in bunks, one above the other, and a double bed against the front wall. The bed was spread with an Army blanket. I put the lamp down on a small table and went back out to the car.

I carried her in and put her on the bed. Her face was waxen white in the lamplight and her hair was a dark mist across the pillow. She must have been at least thirty, she was a passed-out drunk, but she was the most beautiful thing I had ever seen. I stood looking down at her for a minute. The whole thing was a lousy mess. Then I shrugged and picked up the lamp. I wasn't her mother. And it was a rough world, any way you looked at it.

I built a fire in the cookstove and went up to the spring for a couple of buckets of water. It was full light now, and lovely, with bluish-gray smoke curling out of the stovepipe above the old shake roof and going off into the sky through the trees. I moved the car into the old shed on the far side of the house and closed the doors. Then I took an inventory of the food supply. Bill always kept the kitchen well stocked. There were a couple of boxes of canned stuff in the storeroom and some flour and miscellaneous staples in the cup-boards. I opened a fresh can of coffee and put on the coffeepot.

I sat down and smoked a cigarette, listening to the crackle of the fire and realizing I felt tired after being on the run all night. Drawing a hand across my face, I felt the rasp of beard stubble, and went over to the mirror hanging on the rear wall. I looked like a thug. My eyebrows and hair are blond, but when the beard comes out it's ginger-colored and dirty.

I rooted around in the storeroom until I found somebody's duffel bag with a toilet kit in it. It held a safety razor and some blades, but no shaving soap. I used hand soap to lather up, and shaved. Then I put the shirt and tie back on. It was a little better.

The coffee had started to boil. It smelled good. I poured a cup and sat down to smoke another cigarette. The sun was coming up now. I thought of all that had happened since this time yesterday morning. Everything had changed.

I no longer worried about the fact that I was breaking laws as fast as they could set them up in the gallery. My only concern was that what I was doing was dangerous as hell and if I was caught I was ruined. But it was not even that which caused the chill goose flesh across my shoulders.

It was the thought of that money, more money than I could earn in a lifetime. It lay somewhere just beyond the reach of my fingers, and I could feel the fingers itching as they stretched out toward it. Mrs. Butler knew where it was.

And I had Mrs. Butler.

It was nearly two hours before I heard her move on the bed in the other room. She was coming around.

I'd better be good now. I had to be good to make this stick. I picked up the bottle of whisky and a glass, and went in.

Chapter Five

She was sitting up on the bed with her hands on each side of her face, the fingers running up into her hair. It was the first time I had ever seen her eyes, and I could see what Diana James had meant when she said they were big and smoky-looking.

She stared at me.

"Good morning," I said. I poured a drink into the glass.

"Who are you?" she demanded. She looked around the room. "And what am I doing in this place?"

"Better take a little of this," I said. "Or if you'd rather have it, we've got black coffee." I knew damn well which she'd rather have, but I threw in the coffee just to keep talking.

She took the drink. I corked the bottle and went out into the other room with it. When I came back I had a basin of cold water, a washcloth and towel, and her purse. I set them on the table and shoved the table over where she could reach it. She ignored the whole thing.

"Will you answer my question?" she said. "What am I doing in this revolting shanty?"

"Oh," I said. "Then you don't remember?"

"Certainly not. And I never saw you before."

"We'll get to that in a minute," I said. "Right now I just want you to feel better."

I squeezed out the cloth and handed it to her. She scrubbed at her face with it and I gave her the towel. Then I dug her comb out of the jumble of stuff in her purse. I watched her comb her hair. It wasn't quite black in daylight. It was rich, dark brown.

"How about some coffee?" I said.

She stood up and brushed at the blue robe. I nodded toward the door and followed her into the other room. She sat down in the chair I pulled out for her. I poured some coffee and then gave her a cigarette and lit it. Then I sat down across from her, straddling a chair with my arms across the back.

She ignored the coffee. "Perhaps you can explain this," she said.

I frowned. "Don't you remember anything at all?"

"No."

"I was hoping you would," I said. "Especially what happened before I got there."

"I don't know what you're talking about," she said. "And will you, for the love of the merciful God, tell me who you are?"

"Barton," I said. "John Barton, of Globe Surety. Remember? I'm from the Kansas City office, but they put me on it because I used to work out of Sanport and know this country."

I had to keep snowing her. She was rum-dum, but she still might be sharp enough to want to see something that said Barton, of Globe Surety Company. The thing was to give her the impression I'd already shown her my credentials but that she'd been drunk when she'd seen them. We wouldn't mention that. It would be embarrassing.

But she didn't go for the fake hand-off. She came right in and smeared me. "I've never heard of a company by that name," she said. "And I never saw you before in my life. How do I know who you are?"

It was the longest, coldest bluff I had ever pulled in my life, and if I didn't make it stick I was penitentiary bait. I felt empty all the way down to my legs.

"Oh, sure," I said. I reached back for the wallet in my hip pocket and started flipping through the leaves of identification stuff. I made a show of finding the one I wanted, and just as I started to pass her the whole thing, I said, "Can you remember anything at all about what he looked like? Even his general build would help."

She took her eyes off the wallet and looked at me. "Who looked like?" she asked blankly.

"The man you said tried to kill you. Just before I got there."

That did it.

She gasped. And just for an instant I saw fear in her eyes. Then it was gone. "Tried to kill me?"

"Yes," I said, still crowding her. "I realize it was dark, of course. But did he say anything when he lunged at you? I mean, would you recognize his voice?"

"I don't even know what you're talking about," she said. "I was just up in my room—"

"That's right," I interrupted. I put the wallet back in my pocket while I went on talking. "You were playing the phonograph, you said. And when I found you out

there on the lawn you had a record in your hand. I
don't think you even knew you were carrying it, but I
couldn't get it away from you. You had a death grip on
it. At first I couldn't make any sense at all out of what
you were trying to say."

She shook her head. "I don't remember any of it,"
she said. "Maybe you'd better tell me what happened."

"Sure." I lit a cigarette for myself. "I had to talk to
you. We're trying to run down a lead our Sanport
office dug up—but I'll get to that in a minute. Anyway,
I got into Mount Temple last night after midnight, and
when I'd checked into the hotel I tried to call you. The
line was busy. I tried again later, and it was the same
thing, so I got a cab and went out to your house.

"And just as I was coming up the drive in the cab I
saw you in the headlights. You had run out the front
door and were going around toward the garage. When
I got over to where you were, you had fallen on the
lawn. You had this phonograph record in one hand and
your purse in the other. You were in a panic, and practically hysterical. I couldn't make out what you were
trying to say at first. It was something about listening
to the music in your room by candlelight, and that you
had looked around over your shoulder and there was a
man standing behind you. I tried to calm you down
and get the story straightened out, but you just kept
saying the same thing over and over—that the man
had lunged at you with something in his hand.

"You didn't seem to know how you'd got away from
him, but when I suggested we go inside you started to
go to pieces. Nothing could make you go back inside
the house. All you wanted to do was get in the car and

get away. I was afraid we'd wake the neighbors, so I went along with it. I drove, and tried to figure out what to do. I couldn't take you to the hotel or a tourist court there in town, of course, because you'd be known everywhere. You went to sleep, and I finally thought of this place. It's a duck club I belonged to when I was in Sanport and I knew there wouldn't be anybody out here this time of year. Maybe you could get some rest, and we could talk it over when you woke up. That's about it.

"I wish you could remember something about that man, though. If he was trying to kill you, he may get you next time."

She didn't say anything for a moment. Her eyes were thoughtful.

"Do you have any idea who he could have been?" I asked.

"No," she said. "Do you really think I saw anybody?"

"Yes," I said. Baby, I thought, if you only knew. "Yes. I think you did. You were under a terrible strain."

"I must have been." She stared moodily down at her hands. When she looked back up at me she said, "You said you came to talk to me. What about?"

"Your husband."

"Oh." She sighed. "I suppose you want to ask some more questions. Or the same ones over again. I've told it so many times…"

"Yes," I said. I felt good. I'd put it over. "It's been rough on you, and we hate to be the pests we are, but we've got a job to do. However, mine isn't quite the same as the police's. They're looking for your husband."

"Aren't you?" she asked.

I studied the end of the cigarette. "Only incidentally."

"What do you mean?"

"I'll be frank with you, Mrs. Butler. My orders, first and last, are to find that money. Any way I can. We have to pick up the tab for it if it's not recovered, so you can see where our interest is."

"I wish I could help you. You can see that, can't you? But there isn't anything I can tell you that hasn't already been told."

I waited, not saying anything.

She sighed again. "All right. He came home from the bank at noon that Saturday, said he was going to some lake in Louisiana, fishing, and that he'd be home Sunday night. I didn't see any money, or anything that could have held that much money, but maybe it was in the car, if he had it. He didn't take any clothes except fishing clothes, as far as I could tell afterward. I know he didn't take a bag. Just the fishing tackle. I was a little worried when he didn't return Sunday night, but I thought perhaps he had merely decided to stay over another day. And then, Monday morning, Mr. Matthews, the president of the bank, came out and told me—" She quit talking and just stared down at her hands.

"You don't have any idea why he would do a thing like that?" I asked.

The hesitation was hardly noticeable. "No," she said.

I frowned at the cigarette in my hand, and then looked squarely at her. "Well, I'm afraid we do now," I said. "It's unpleasant, and I wish I didn't have to be the one to tell you."

"What do you mean?"

"He was running off with another woman."

"No!"

"I'm sorry, Mrs. Butler. But that's the lead I mentioned, the thing our Sanport office found out. The girl's name is Diana James, or at least that's what she calls herself. She had an apartment in Sanport, and that's where he was headed. She was going to hide him there."

"I don't believe it!"

"Unfortunately, it's true."

"Then," she said, "under the circumstances, don't you think you're just wasting your time talking to me? Apparently this James person is the only one who really knows anything about my husband."

"No," I said. "It's not quite as simple as that. You see, he never did get to her apartment. And the only answer to that is a very ugly one."

She was watching me narrowly. "What?"

"I'm sorry, Mrs. Butler. But he's dead, and has been ever since that Saturday."

She tried to get up from the chair, but her legs wouldn't hold her and she slumped onto the table. I carried her into the other room and put her on the bed. In a moment her eyes opened. She just lay there looking up at the rafters. She didn't cry.

I went out to the other room and got the bottle. It had gone all right so far. She knew now that at least one outfit was wise to the fact that Butler had never reached the James girl's apartment, and had guessed why he hadn't. Maybe not the police, but the insurance company was working with them, wasn't it?

"I'm sorry," I said. I held out the drink. "This will make you feel better."

She sat up and brushed the dark hair back from her face with her hand. She drank the whisky and shuddered.

"You must have suspected it," I said. "After all, it's been over two months, with the police in twenty states looking for him."

"I suppose so," she said. "Maybe I just didn't want to admit it."

I sat down in the chair and lit her a cigarette. She took it between listless fingers and forgot it.

"You see how that changes the picture, don't you?" I said. "We're not looking for your husband any more. We're looking for whoever killed him. That is, the police are, or will be as soon as they get the word about the James girl. What I'm looking for is the money. And that brings us to why I wanted to talk to you. You might be able to add something."

"What do you mean?"

"I mean you might think of something that didn't seem important before, but that might be significant now in view of this. Was there somebody who could have found out he was going to do it? Was there somebody who knew about Diana James? You see the jealousy angle, don't you? I mean—he had one girl-friend that we know of, so there might have been another."

"I understand he was also married," she said. "But go on."

"Believe me, Mrs. Butler, I don't enjoy this either.

But my orders are to find that money. The police are going to have their hands full trying to find a murderer, and building a case that'll stand up in court." I paused just a second; then I added, "I'm not interested in that angle of it."

"You're not?"

"No. Let's look at it objectively. Up to the point of recovering the money and prosecuting the man who stole it, our jobs overlap. But if the man is dead, he's beyond the reach of prosecution, so when we get the money back we're out of it. That may sound callous to you, but it's only sound business. The police are paid to solve murders; we're not."

I stopped. It was very quiet in the room.

"You see what I mean, don't you?" I said.

She nodded slowly. "Yes. I understand perfectly." She paused, and then added, "They must pay you well."

"Well enough. But, again, it's strictly business, if you look at it in the right way. I don't think your husband was killed for that money. The motive was jealousy, and the money didn't have anything to do with it. That being the case, we're not involved. We get back what belongs to us. We drop it. You see?"

"And if you don't get it back?"

"Then it's a different story. People's emotional explosions don't interest us until they start costing us a hundred and twenty thousand dollars an explosion. Then we're in it up to the neck, and we get rough about it."

She nodded again. "Yes. I can see you would feel quite unclean if you ever became contaminated with an emotion."

"It's a job. Like pumping gas, or being vice-president of a bank. If I want to be emotional, I do it on my own time."

She said nothing. She just continued to watch me.

I leaned forward a little and tapped her on the wrist, "But let's get back to what we were talking about. Catching your husband would have been easy, if somebody hadn't killed him. We'd have had that money back by now except that a clear-cut case of embezzlement got loused up with some jealous woman blowing her stack. She's just making it tough for me—and for no reason at all, because she didn't want the money in the first place. And when I find out who she is I can make it tough for her. Or she can get off the hook by being sensible. You see how simple it is?"

"Yes," she said. "It is very simple. Isn't it?"

She smiled. And then she hit me as hard as she could across the mouth.

Chapter Six

"Now that I've answered your question," she said coolly, "perhaps you'll answer one for me. What were you doing in my house?"

It had been too sudden. Even without having your mouth bounced off your teeth, it was a little hard to keep up. "I just told you."

The big smoke-blue eyes were perfectly self-possessed now. "I know. You said I was wandering around on the lawn with a phonograph record in my hand, which isn't a bad extension of the actual truth. So you must have been up there in my room when I was listening to the phonograph."

"You don't believe me?"

"Certainly not. I know what I did. I went to sleep. And just in case you think I'm bluffing, I can even tell you the last recording I played before I dropped off. It was Handel's *Water Music Suite*. Wasn't it?"

"How would I know?" I said.

"You probably wouldn't, at that. But just who are you? And what is your business, besides extortion?"

I was catching up a little. "Don't throw your weight around too much," I said. "Suppose the police started wondering just why his car showed up right in front of Diana James's apartment."

"Did it?" she asked.

"You know damned well it did."

She shook her head. "No. But it does have a certain element of poetic justice, doesn't it?"

It was odd, but I believed her. About that part of it, anyway.

"I'm beginning to understand now," she said, studying me thoughtfully through the cigarette smoke. "How *is* the accessible Miss James? As bountiful as ever, I hope?"

"She likes you too," I said.

She smiled. "We adore each other. But I do wish she would stop sending people up here to tear my house apart."

I remembered the slashed cushions. "So that's who—"

"You didn't think there was anything original about it, did you? I can assure you that in almost nothing connected with Miss James are you likely to be the first."

I said nothing. I was busy with a lot of things. She knew the house had been searched before, but still she hadn't reported it to the police. That meant she couldn't, and that I was still right. She was in whatever it was right up to her neck. She couldn't report me either.

Her eyes were slightly mocking. "But I see you admit you had started to search the place. What changed your mind? I was asleep and wouldn't bother you."

"It got a little crowded," I said. "With three of us."

"Three?"

"The other one was the man who tried to kill you."

"Oh, we're going back to that again?"

"Listen," I said. I told her what had happened.

"You don't expect me to believe that?" she asked when I had finished.

"When you go back to the house, take a look at what's left of your records and the player. We rolled on 'em. The other guy was a heavyweight, too."

"He was?" she asked. She was thinking about it. Then she shrugged it off. "I don't believe you."

"Suit yourself," I said.

Then I stopped. We had both heard it. It was a car crossing that wooden culvert at the edge of the meadow. It came on, and pulled to a stop right in front of the porch. I could hear the brakes squeak.

I shook my head savagely and motioned for her to stay where she was. She couldn't be seen through the front window. I stepped out into the other room. The coat, with the gun in it, was on the back of a chair against the other wall. As I started across I could look out the front door and see the car. There was only one person in it, and it was a girl. I could hear the radio, crooning softly.

I went out and walked around the car to the driver's side. She smiled. She was an ash blonde with an angelic face and a cool pair of eyes, and you knew she could turn on the honey-chile like throwing a switch at Boulder Dam. She turned it on.

"Good moarornin'," she said. It came out slowly and kept falling on you like honey dripping out of a spoon. "It's absolutely the *silliest* thing, but I think I'm lost."

"Yes?" I said. She was eight miles from a county road and twenty from the highway. And she didn't look much like a bird watcher. "What are you looking for?"

She poured another jug of it over me. "A farm-house. It's a man named Mr. Gillespie. They said to go out this road, and take that road, and turn over here, and go down that way, you know how people tell you to go somewhere, they just get you all mixed up, it's the *silliest* thing. Actually. All these roads with no names on them, how do you know which one they *mean?*"

Maybe I imagined it, but the patter and the eyes didn't seem to match. And the eyes were looking around.

The radio had quit crooning and was talking. I didn't pay any attention to it. Not then.

"Did they tell you to go through a gate?" I asked.

"Oh, yes, definitely a gate. Mr. Cramer, he's the manager of the store, he was the one that found out Mr. Gillespie had forgotten to sign one of the time-payment papers when he bought the cookstove and took it home in his truck. Anyway, he definitely said a gate, and then about a mile after the gate you turn— I know you're not Mr. Gillespie, are you? You don't look a bit like him."

"No," I said. "My name's Graves. I'm on a fishing trip."

"My," she said admiringly, looking at the white shirt and the tie, "you go fishing all dressed up, don't you? My brother, when he goes fishing, he's the messiest thing, actually, you should see him."

"I just got here," I said. "A few minutes ago."

Her story was plausible enough. She might be looking for somebody named Gillespie. God knows, she sounded as if she could get lost. She could get lost in a telephone booth, or a double bed. But still...

An icicle walked slowly up my spine and sat down between my shoulder blades.

It was the radio. It was what the radio was saying.

"...Butler..."

"Are you fishing all alone?" Dreamboat asked.

All I had to do was stand there in the sunlight beside the car and try to hear what the radio was saying, and remember it, and listen to this pink-and-silver idiot, and answer in the right places, and at the same time try to figure out whether she was an idiot or not and what she was really up to, and keep her from noticing I was paying any attention to the radio.

"Mrs. Madelon Butler, thirty-three, lovely brunette widow of the missing bank official sought since last June eighth..."

Widow. So they'd found his body.

"Mrs. Butler is believed to have fled in a blue 1953 Cadillac."

"I don't see any car," she said, looking around. "How did you get here?"

"...sought in connection with the murder. Police in neighboring states have been alerted, and a description of Mrs. Butler and the license number of the car..."

"Pickup truck," I said. "It's in the shed."

"...since the discovery of the body late yesterday, but no trace of the missing money has been found. Police are positive, however, that the apprehension of Mrs. Butler will clear up..."

The man had known the body'd been found, and

that they were going to arrest her. He didn't want her arrested. He still didn't. Maybe this lost blonde wasn't lost.

"Malenkov," the radio said.

But she was going to get lost, and damned fast.

"—drink of water," she was saying. She was smiling at me. She wanted to come into the house. She wanted to look around.

I smiled at her. "Sure, baby. But water? Look, I got bourbon."

I was leaning in the window a little. I slid her skirt up.

"Thought I saw an ant on your stocking," I said. I patted a handful of bare, pink-candy thigh. "Come on in, Blondie."

The "You—" was as cold and deadly as a rifle shot. Then she got back into character. "*Well!* I must say!"

But the only thing she could do, under the circumstances, was go. She went.

I took a deep breath and watched the car go across the meadow and into the timber, and then I could hear it climbing the hill in second gear. It didn't stop. I heard it die away in the distance.

He might be out there in the timber somewhere with his gun, or he might be still in town. Maybe he'd just sent her scouting. If that had been his car following us last night, he had finally figured out where we'd turned off, and he knew we had to be back in this country somewhere.

Well, there was a lot of it. They had plenty of places to look.

Unless, I thought coldly...Maybe she had seen

through that old varsity fumble and knew I was just trying to get rid of her. Maybe she knew she had already found what she was looking for.

There was one way to find out. That was to stand out here in the open like a goof until he got back with the gun and shot a hole in my head. I went inside.

Madelon Butler had come out of the bedroom and was standing by the table where the bottle was. She turned and watched me.

"Could you hear the radio?" I asked.

She shook her head. "Why?"

"You'd better sit down. There at the end of the table, where you can't be seen from outside. And take a drink. You're going to need it."

She sat down. "What is it now?"

"They've found your husband's body. And the police are looking for you."

She poured the drink and smiled at me. "You do have a flair for melodrama, don't you?"

"You think I'm lying?"

"Certainly. And who was this timely courier, bringing the news? An accomplice?"

I sat down where I could see out the door and across the meadow. "Look. See if you can get this through your supercilious head. You're in a jam. One hell of a jam. Nobody brought any news. It was on the radio, in that car. The police are looking for you, for murder. And not only that, but the girl in the car was looking for you too."

I told her about it.

She listened boredly until I had finished; then all she did was reach for her purse and take out a mirror and some make-up stuff. She splashed crimson onto her mouth. In spite of myself, I watched her. She was arrogant and conceited as hell, but when you looked away from her for a moment and then looked back you went through it all over again. You didn't believe anybody could be that beautiful.

"I'm ready to go back to town," she said, "if you are."

"Don't you want to hear me waste my breath any more?"

"Frankly, no. I should think we'd about run through your repertoire."

"You don't believe any of it at all?"

She put the finishing touches on the lips, pressed them together, looked in the mirror once more, and then across at me. She smiled. "Don't be ridiculous. By your own admission, you're a housebreaker, liar, and impostor. And attempted extortionist. Quite an array of talent, I'll admit; but to ask me to believe you is a little insulting, wouldn't you say?"

I leaned across the table and caught her wrist. "And don't forget abduction, while you're adding it up. So why don't you have me arrested, if you don't believe any of it?"

"And add to the burden of the taxpayers?"

"No," I said. "I'll tell you why. You can't."

"Don't paw me," she said.

I reached over and took the other wrist. I slid my hands up inside the wide sleeves of the robe and held her arms above the elbows. "I want that money. And I'm going to get it. Why don't you use your head? Alone, you haven't got a chance, and the money's no good to you if you're dead. Maybe I can save you."

"Save me from what?" she asked coldly.

I shook my head and took my hands off her arms to light a cigarette. "Has your car got a radio in it?"

"Yes. Why?"

"I'll tell you the easy way to find out if I'm telling the truth. Trying to go back to town is the hard way, and there's only one to a customer. In about an hour there should be some more news. We'll listen to it."

"Maybe there's some on now," she said. She picked up her purse and started toward the door. She had a good start before I realized what she was up to.

I jumped after her. By the time I reached the door she had run down off the porch and was standing in the open, fumbling in the purse for her keys and looking around for the car.

"Wait!" I yelled. She paid no attention.

She swung her face around and saw the shed at the side of the house. The car had to be in there. She whirled, ran one step toward it, and then it happened.

The purse sailed out of her hands as if a hurricane had grabbed it. She stopped abruptly and stared as it flopped crazily and landed six feet away from her on the edge of the porch, and we both heard the deadly *whuppp!* as something slammed into the front wall of the house.

She was frozen there. I was down off the porch and running toward her before I heard the sound of the gun. Without even thinking about it, I knew it was a rifle and that he was shooting from somewhere beyond the meadow, over two hundred yards away. She started to run now. I grabbed her. It was four long strides back to the front step. I dug in, feeling my whole back draw up into one icy knot. I was a hundred yards wide, and all target.

I leaped onto the porch. I stumbled, and slammed in through the open doorway, trying to keep from falling on her. And just as we hit the floor I saw a coffee cup on the table ahead of us explode into nothing, like a soap bubble. The pieces rained onto the floor.

I rolled her over me to get us out of the doorway, and reached back with one foot to kick the door shut. He put another one through it just as it closed. A golden splinter tore off the wood on the inside, and on the back wall a frying pan hanging on a nail bounced and clanged to the floor.

It was silent now except for the quick sob of her breath. We lay on the floor with our faces only inches apart. The fright was leaving her eyes now, and I could see comprehension in them, and a growing coldness.

"Maybe you'd like an affidavit with that," I said.

I pushed myself up from the floor. She was trying to sit up. One side of her face was covered with dust, and a trickle of blood from a splinter scratch was almost black against the pale column of her throat.

"Stay where you are," I said. I scooted over and stood up beside the front window. Peering out one corner of it, I could see the meadow. It was completely deserted and peaceful in the sunlight. Somewhere beyond, in the dark line of timber at the foot of the hill, he lay with his rifle and waited for something to move.

He probably wouldn't try to come any closer. Not until tonight. But in the meantime nobody would go out that road.

Chapter Seven

"The stupid idiot," she said. I looked around. She was standing up, squarely in line between the front and rear windows. I didn't say anything. I dived.

I hit her just at the waist and took her down with me, turning a little to land on my shoulder. Splinters raked through my shirt. Panes in the front and rear windows blew up at the same time and glass tinkled on the floor.

"What's the matter with you?" she spat at me. "Are you crazy?"

She lay beside me, caught in my arms like a beautiful and enraged wildcat. I disengaged an arm, picked a sliver of windowpane off the front of her robe, held it up so she could see it, and tossed it toward the front window. Her eyes followed it.

"Oh," she said.

"If you feel like silhouetting yourself again," I said, "tell me where that money is first. You won't need it."

"What can we do?" she asked.

"Several things, I suppose, if I didn't have to spend all my time knocking you down. Do you think you can stay here this time?"

"Yes."

"All right."

I crawled over her. When I was away from the

windows I stood up and ran into the bedroom. Grabbing a couple of blankets off one of the bunks, I draped one across the bedroom window and brought the other out.

I stood beside the rear window. "Cover your face," I said. "We're going to have more glass."

She put an arm over her face. I flipped the blanket. It caught over the old curtain rod. Glass smashed in the front window again and the blanket jerked, but remained on the rod. It had a hole in it.

I looked swiftly around. The back door was locked, the window covered now. The storeroom had no outside door, no window. He could sneak around to the sides or back, but he couldn't see in anywhere to shoot. And he knew I had his gun.

From that distance he probably couldn't see in the front window now, with no light behind it. *Maybe* he couldn't, I thought. I could put another blanket over it, but I wanted to be able to see out on one side, at least. The thought of being sealed up in there with no way to guess where he was didn't appeal to me.

"Is it all right now?" she asked.

"No. Stay down."

I looked at her again, and thought of something.

"Take off that robe," I said.

She sat on the floor and stared coldly at me. "Don't we have anything better to do?"

"You have got something on under it, haven't you?"

"Yes. Pajamas."

"Well, shut up and toss it here."

She shrugged and slid out of it, turning a little to get it out from under her. The pajamas were blue and wide-sleeved, the lounging type. She tossed the robe. I crawled over and stood up beside the front window and flipped it over the curtain rod. It slid off. I picked it up and tried again. This time I got more of it over the rod and it stuck. There was no shot.

I stepped back. It was fine. It was just sheer enough to be transparent with the light on the other side. I could see the meadow. Nothing stirred.

"All right," I said. "He can't see in."

She stood up. "What do we do now?"

"I don't know."

I went over and got the gun out of my coat. I slid the clip out and looked at it. There was one cartridge in it. Two, I thought, with the one in the chamber.

"We can't just stay here," she said.

"You got a better idea?" I checked the safety again and shoved the gun in my belt.

I fished in my pocket for a cigarette. The pack was empty. I went over to the coat and got another. I opened it, and gave her one. We sat down at the table. I could see out across the meadow without being directly behind the window.

"Couldn't we sneak out the back door and get to the car?" she asked.

"Sure," I said. "You might even get it out of the shed before he killed you. You've seen him shoot that rifle."

She said nothing.

"And," I went on, "suppose you did get out to the highway? What then? Every cop in the state has the description and license number of that Cadillac."

She stared thoughtfully at me through the smoke. "Afoot? Out the back door?"

"It's twenty miles to the nearest place you could catch a bus. You're a dish everybody looks at. And you're wearing pajamas and bedroom slippers. Any more ideas?"

"Charming thug, aren't you? Shall I cheer you up for a while now?"

"Why? I'm all right. Nobody knows me; I can still run."

"Well? Why don't you?"

"You don't scare much, do you?"

"Would being scared do any good?"

"You're about the hardest citizen I've ever run into," I said. "Did you kill Butler alone, or did that guy out there help you? Is that how he got in the act?"

"I don't know anything about it."

"Which one of you has the money?"

"I have nothing to say."

"Who was that girl in the car? Angel-faced ash blonde, with a hush-puppy accent."

"Why didn't you ask her?"

"I don't think she liked me."

"I can understand that," she said.

"Well, you're popular," I said. "You're in great demand."

She put the cigarette in the ashtray and leaned back in the chair with her hands clasped behind her head. The pajama sleeves slid down her arms. They were lovely arms.

I watched her, thinking swiftly. We were both in one hell of a jam, but I was beginning to get the glimmerings of an idea. It all depended on whether she had the money or not, and I still believed she had it.

There was no use even trying to guess whether she had killed Butler, or whether that man out there had, or both of them; but I was beginning to respect the cool and deadly intelligence behind that lovely face, and I was growing more convinced of one thing all the time: that no matter who had killed him, unless that guy out there was a lot smarter than I thought he was, *she* was the one that had the money. It figured that way.

"You're the Homecoming Queen," I said. "Everybody wants you."

"I really don't see what you're waiting around for," she said. "You have pointed out that there is no possibility of escape. I agree with you. Any further discussion of it is superfluous; and you should realize, if it's entertainment you're after, that taunting me with it is futile."

I leaned back in the chair and blew a smoke ring. "I was going to make you an offer."

"What kind of offer?"

"It doesn't matter. If you haven't got that money, I'd just be wasting my breath."

She smiled. "You know," she said, "there is a touching sort of simplicity about you I almost admire. Anyone with a less comprehensive stupidity might get sidetracked once in a while and wander off the main objective, but you never do. You started out to get that money, and by God, you're going to get it. I almost regret that you won't."

"Well, if you haven't got it, what's the use talking about it?"

She shook her head. "It isn't a question of whether I have it or not. The real point—as anyone but a thick-

headed mastodon would have figured out hours ago—
is that if I did have it I'd willingly go to hell before I'd
see Diana James get a nickel of it."

I put down the cigarette and stared at her. So that was
what had been holding up the negotiations. You never
knew. They didn't make sense; they never did, not even
the smart ones. Not even to save her own skin…

"Look," I said. "The hell with Diana James. Haven't
you heard? She's been scratched."

"What do you mean?"

"Just that. She double-crossed me before we even
started. She told me you were in Sanport, to get me to
come up here and shake down the house. What did
she care if I got caught?"

"And that isn't quite all," she said. "Think again."

"How's that?"

"You still haven't seen the full beauty of it. Suppose
I had surprised you and you'd got rattled and killed
me? Wouldn't that have been tragic?"

I thought about it. The fact that I wouldn't have
been stupid enough to do a crazy thing like that was
beside the point. Diana James could easily have been
counting on the possibility.

"Well," I said. "That's how it is with you friend Miss
James. She's been dropped from the rolls."

"I see," she said coolly. "And now you're ready to
transfer your greathearted devotion?"

I walked over and took a good look out the window.
The meadow was empty of life. I came back and
sat down.

"Yes," I said.

"I'm flattered."

"Never mind you're flattered. Have you got the money?"

"I might have," she said.

"Where is it?"

"I said I *might* have."

"It'll take more than that, honey," I said. "Let's get it on the line."

"Why?"

"You haven't got a chance. You're cold meat. As soon as it's dark and I can get out of here, I'm going to shove. I can get away. And you'll be a dead woman with a hundred and twenty thousand dollars as soon as your friend out there moves in on you."

She stared thoughtfully. "And what is this proposition of yours?"

"The geetus, baby."

"I have it."

"You know about not trying to kid me, don't you?"

Her eyes were cold. "I said I had it."

I took another drag on the cigarette and looked at her a long time. There was no hurry. Keep the pressure on her. "Let's put it this way," I said at last. "You're dead. We both know that. You're dead twice. If that character out there doesn't clobber you with his rifle, you'll be caught by the police and go on trial for murder. With your looks and a good sob story you might beat the chair and get off with life, but it's a sad outlook either way.

"Alone, you haven't got a prayer. No car, no clothes, no place to hide. You're naked, with the light shining on you. With me helping, you might have a chance. A slim one. Say one in a thousand.

"My deal is the same one Diana James and your husband cooked up. I'll try to get you out of here, hide you until some of the pressure is off and we can redecorate you as a blonde or redhead, and deliver you to the West Coast or somewhere. I don't say I can do it. You can see the odds yourself. But I'll try."

She nodded slowly. "I see. And for how much?"

"Make it a round number. Say a hundred and twenty thousand dollars."

She continued to stare at me. "You know, when you said I was hard, I didn't realize what an authority I was listening to."

"You didn't think I was going to do it for nothing? Look at the risk. The minute I start to help you, I'm committing a crime myself. And when I lose my amateur standing it's going to be for big money."

"So you'd just take all of it?"

"That's right. Of course, if you get a better offer in the next hour or so..."

"And what would I live on if I did get to the Coast?"

"What does anybody live on? Go to work."

"At what? I never did any work in my life."

"How do I know what? I'm not an employment counselor. Is it a deal, or isn't it?"

She thought about it for a minute. Then she shrugged. "All right. But suppose you get the money? What guarantee do I have that you'll carry out your end of it? Just your innate sense of honor?"

"That's right."

"Enchanting prospect, isn't it?"

"Yeah," I said. "Now, where's the money?"

She smiled. "That's the only thing I have in my

favor. You'll have to go through with at least part of your bargain before you even get it."

"Why?"

"It's in three safe-deposit boxes in Sanport."

"Safe-deposit boxes!" I stared at her. "Well, how in the name of God are you going to get at it? With every cop in the state looking for you!"

"Well, naturally, they're not rented under my right name."

"Oh," I said. "And where are the keys?"

"At home."

"In your house?"

She nodded, her eyes a little mocking.

"But that means that even if we can find some way to get out of here, we've still got to go right back in the lion's mouth."

"Umh-humh," she said. "It isn't easy, is it? But that's the reason I engaged such high-priced talent. It's no job for the inept. Let me know when you think of something."

The sun climbed higher. It was hot in the cabin. I tried to make myself sit still and think, but then I'd be up and pacing the floor again. I watched the window constantly.

There was a way out of it. There had to be. All I had to do was find it. We had to have a car. We couldn't use her Caddy, but there was another car down there somewhere. He had one. But he also had a rifle, and he knew how to use it.

"Do you suppose he's gone?" she asked. She was still sitting at the table, finishing another drink.

"Of course not," I said. "He's just waiting. We have to move sometime, and when we move he lets us have it."

"How does he know we haven't sneaked out the back door and left on foot?"

"Because," I explained curtly, "he knows how you're dressed. He knows you're not going anywhere without a car. And we can't use the Cadillac, even if he wasn't watching it with a gun."

She poured another drink. The bottle was nearly empty. She held up the glass and looked at it. "Well, you're the high-priced expert."

She was chromium-plated and solid ice both ways from the middle. From her attitude you'd think she was merely a spectator at all this. It was something she was watching from the first row balcony and finding a little tiresome.

The air was clammy with heat. My shirt stuck to me. I looked at her and the bottle with irritation. "Look. You can lay off that sauce."

She glanced briefly up at me. "And you can mind your own business."

I sat down across from her. I caught the front of her pajamas and pulled her up straight in the chair. "Let's get this straight. Right now. If we get out of here, for about the next two months I'm going to have the job of trying to hide you from the police. It's going to be rough, believe me. And if you get caught I'm in the bucket too. So I don't intend to make the job any harder by having to watch out for a blabber-mouthed lush wandering around in a fog. You'll stay sober."

There was only faint interest in her face, as if she

were just waiting for me to crawl back under a rock. "If you're certain you've finished," she said, "you might take your hands off my clothing."

"Yes, Empress," I said. I shoved her back in the chair. "But keep it in mind."

"Do you intend doing anything about getting us out of here?"

"I'm working on it, Your Highness. But we can't go anywhere until after dark, anyway. So keep your pants on."

"Barbarian."

"Who is that guy out there?"

"How would I know? He hasn't sent in his card."

"Cut it out. Who is he?"

"I fail to see where it concerns you. You're being paid to neutralize him, not identify him."

"Boyfriend?"

"As you wish," she said boredly.

"Who killed Butler? Both of you?"

She made no answer. She merely stared at the empty space where I would have been sitting if I hadn't already crawled back under the rock.

Even if we got out of here, I thought…

Living with her for two months was going to be fun. Which one of us would start to come unglued first?

Chapter Eight

I stood with my back against the rear window and stared out the front. As nearly as I could, I lined up the broken panes front and rear, and sighted. He'd be right in there somewhere. There was no reason for him to move, if he could see everything from where he was. He could watch the house there, and he could cover the road.

There was nothing to mark his spot, however. One area in the timber was just like any other. I looked farther up the hill. On the skyline and a little to the right I saw a tall tree that had apparently been struck by lightning. That would serve as a reference point.

"What are you doing?" she asked.

"Getting ready to call a cab," I said.

I took off the white shirt. It could be seen too easily in the timber. I found an old blue one in the storeroom and put it on, and shoved the gun back in my belt.

She was still watching me. I went over to the table, picked up the bottle of whisky, and poured what was left on the floor.

"You're going to have to be at least partly sober for this," I said. "Now. The only reason he hasn't walked in here and shot you is that he knows I'm here and that I've got a gun. It's his gun. You still following me?"

She nodded, saying nothing.

"Well, I'm going out there. I'm going to try to get behind him. I hope I can get out the back without being seen. But the gimmick is that he might not shoot if he did see me. It's you he wants. So he may pretend he doesn't see me, and let me go. And when I'm out there on the wide part of the swing he may come in for you.

"The front door is locked. After I go out, bolt the back one. Sit in the storeroom, because it hasn't got any windows. And if you hear him on the porch or if he starts to kick in one of these other windows, scream. And keep screaming. Close the door to the storeroom and pile everything in there against it. And if you smell smoke, scream twice as loud."

"Smoke?"

"That's right. It's one way."

She got it, but it didn't scare her much. "All right," she said. "And thank you for your solicitude. It's touching."

"Isn't it," I said.

I opened the back door and stepped out. Nothing happened.

I dropped off the porch and ran bent over toward the bushes at the edge of the water, the muscles bunched up and icy in the middle of my back. Guessing where he was and what he'd do was fine on paper, but out here in the open I could feel the cross hairs of a telescope sight crawling all over me like long-legged spiders. It was the dead silence all around and not ever knowing that made it bad.

I hit the bushes and dropped into them. A mosquito buzzed around my face and got in my nose. I stifled the impulse to sneeze, and searched the timber along the lake shore in both directions, turning my head very slowly. Nothing moved. I looked behind me, out across the lake, just for the sheer relief of seeing one place he couldn't be. It was glassy under the sun. Out in the middle a mud hen swam, jerking its head, and left a V-shaped ripple on the surface. The trees were dark green along the other shore. It looked like the picture on a sporting-goods calendar.

I started crawling to the right, between the screen of bushes and the water's edge. I had to slide under the little dock where the two skiffs were tied up. I was behind the shed now. A down log blocked my way. I crawled over it. A limb broke, snapping loudly in the hush. I fell to the ground and waited. Nothing happened. Three minutes went by. Four. I started again.

Mud sucked at my hands and knees. Sweat ran down my face. I kept watching for snakes. I looked back. The house and shed were lost in the trees, but I could see the dock. I had come over a hundred yards. A little more would do it. Wherever he was, he'd still be near enough to the edge of the timber to see the whole meadow.

I had to be behind him now. I stood up, wiped some of the mud off my hands, and began slipping through the timber, circling and heading away from the lake. Here in the low ground, underbrush was heavy, but ahead I could see it thinning out as I approached the foot of the hill. I stopped in a minute and held my breath to listen. If he had seen me leave, he'd be closing in now. I'd have to get there fast if she screamed. It was silent except for a squirrel chattering up on the hillside.

The grade began to pitch upward into the pines and stunted post oak. The soil was sandy here and matted in places with pine needles. My feet made no sound at all. I could see the meadow now and then through the trees, two or three hundred yards off to my left and a little below. I went straight up toward the crest of the ridge. In a few minutes I came out on level ground, turned sharp left, and began searching for the tall pine with the dead top. After another hundred yards I found it and faced down toward the lake for a glimpse of the house to orient myself. Through a small opening in the trees I could see part of the roof. I turned ninety degrees and went straight ahead for a hundred and fifty steps, going very slowly now and taking advantage of all the cover I could.

I stopped and squatted down at the foot of a pine. I should be directly above him. Somewhere in the trees below he was lying with his rifle beside him, watching the house. Moving nothing but my eyes, I began covering it foot by foot, every tree trunk, log, bush, every patch of mottled sunlight and shadow. As my eyes probed, I rubbed my hands in the sand and then together, to get the rest of the mud off. I checked the gun in my belt, to be sure it would come free when I needed it.

I could see nothing. No movement, no bit of color that could be clothing. He was farther down. I picked out a clump of bushes ten yards ahead and crept toward it, moving noiselessly on the sand. Crawling up beside it, I lay flat on my stomach and studied the hillside below me for five minutes. There was no sign of him.

I moved again. I could see the edge of the meadow in places below me now and knew this was as far as I could go. If I missed him and got in front of him I was dead. I stopped, lay still, and searched the hillside on both sides and ahead. My eyes made the slow, complete swing from right to left, stopped, and went back again.

I saw him.

I saw a shoe. It grew into a leg and then into two legs half screened by the low-hanging branches of a dogwood twenty yards straight down the hill from where I was. The underbrush was heavier here than it had been on top of the hill, but by moving a little to the right I could see him clearly.

I took a deep breath, feeling tight across the chest. One of us might be dead in the next minute or two. I could try to bluff him with the gun, but suppose he didn't bluff? He was desperate; he had nothing to lose.

I could still go back.

I thought of those three safe-deposit boxes in Sanport and knew there was never any going back now. I started crawling down the hill.

I watched his legs. There was no movement. I could see his whole body now. The rifle, with its telescope sight, lay across a small log in front of him while he watched the clearing and the house. I searched the ground ahead for any leaf or twig that would make the slightest sound if I stepped on it.

Ten feet behind him I straightened up on my knees, pulled the gun out of my belt, leveled it at the back of his head, and said, "All right, Mac. Turn around. Without the gun."

His face jerked around. He started to lift the rifle.

"You'll never make it," I said.

His eyes were a little crazy, but he knew I was right. He didn't have a chance, lying down that way and facing in the other direction.

"Slide the bolt out," I said. "All the way. And throw it—"

I was careless. I'd been intent on him to the exclusion of everything else. It was almost too late when I heard the sound behind me. I started to turn, and the club missed my head just far enough to land on my arm, numbing it out to the fingertips.

He was scrambling to his knees, trying to get the rifle swung around. I clawed at the tree limb with the sick arm and reached back with the other and found her. I put the hand against her belly and threw her at him like a bag of laundry. She took a long step backward and crashed down on top of him and the two of them rolled across the rifle. I reached down for the gun I had dropped.

It was the blonde, but she'd turned off the Southern belle. Her eyes were hot with fury as she untangled her long legs and arms and tried to sit up. She had pine needles in her hair, and a scratch on her knee oozed blood over the ruin of a nylon stocking.

She didn't like me. And you could see the cords in her throat while she was telling me about it.

"Shut up," I said.

I walked over to them. They were both sitting up. The rifle was under her legs in the sand. I pushed them out of the way and dragged it from under her with my foot. She liked me even less. He didn't say anything. He just looked at me with his crazy eyes.

I shoved the rifle backward, stepped back to it, and squatted down. I took the bolt out and threw it twenty yards down the hill into the underbrush. Then I swung the rest of it against a tree. The stock splintered, and broken glass trickled out the end of the 'scope.

"Where's the car?" I said.

Something had been eating him away inside for a long time. You could see it in the hot, crazy eyes, and in the way his hands twitched as he rubbed them across his mouth. "Who are you?" he asked. His voice was ragged. "What do you want?"

"A car," I said. "I thought I mentioned that."

There was something odd about them, and I saw what it was now that I had time to take a good look. They were brother and sister. He was big, and a lot younger, probably not over twenty-one or twenty-two, but it was unmistakable. Maybe it was the identical ash blondness and the well-formed bone structure of their faces. They were good-looking as hell. And full of it.

"You'll never take her out of here," he said. "You'll never take her out of here alive. I'll kill her. I'll kill you."

I gestured with the gun. "On your feet."

He hesitated a moment, watching me; then he got up. She continued to sit there.

I caught her by the arm and hauled her up. Red fingernails slashed toward my face. I brushed her hand away and shoved her. She bounced against him and he caught her to keep her from falling.

"If she won't walk," I said, "carry her."

He stared hungrily at the gun. "Where?"

"Out to the road. We're looking for a car, remember?"

She looked at him with contempt. "Are you afraid of this miserable thug?"

"What do you want me to do?" he said. "He's got the gun."

"So you're going to let her get away?"

"She hasn't got away yet."

"All right, break it up," I said. "You can yak some other time."

"What are you going to do with Mrs. Butler?" she asked.

"I'm going to adopt her. I think she's cute."

"Maybe you don't know what you're getting mixed up in. The police want her for murder. She killed her husband."

"I don't care if she killed Cock Robin," I said. "I just work here. Now shut up and start walking."

They started out toward the road. I kept about six feet behind them. When we struck it we were near the edge of the meadow. I didn't see the car anywhere. It had to be above.

"Turn right," I said. "Up the hill. And stay in the road."

We went silently uphill through the sand.

"You could tell me where it is," I said. "But that would be the easy way. So we'll just walk. It's only eight miles out to the road, and eight miles back."

They made no answer. They walked side by side in icy silence, not looking back.

"If we pass it," I said, "don't bother to say anything. We've got all the rest of the day to walk around."

I watched the ruts, fairly sure I'd see where they had pulled it off the road even if they had it hidden. And just before we reached the crest of the ridge I did. It was pulled off in a clump of dogwood. It was the same car the girl had driven up in.

"Who's got the keys?" I asked.

They stared at me in silent hatred.

It was obvious she didn't have them, because she didn't have a purse. I looked at him. "All right, Blondy. How'd you like one through the leg?"

He took the keys out of his pocket.

"You drive," I said. "And Toots will sit in the middle."

We got in. He backed it out on the road. "Downhill," I said. "To the camp. And don't get any funny ideas about giving it the gun and crashing into a tree. I might walk away from it, but you wouldn't."

We were jammed in together, but I held the gun in my right hand over against the door, where she couldn't grab for it.

She turned her face and stared into mine from a distance of three inches. She was lovely. "You son-of-a-bitch," she said.

I patted her on the leg. "Did you ever find Gillespie, honey?"

Chapter Nine

We stopped in front of the cabin.

I got out. "Inside," I said.

We went up on the porch. I heard Madelon Butler unlocking the door, and knew she had watched us from the window. The door opened and the blonde went in, followed by her brother. I was in the rear, not expecting it, and they almost pulled it off.

He jumped inside, making some kind of hoarse roaring sound in his throat, and the blonde tried to slam and bolt the door ahead of me. I got a foot in it just before it closed, and leaned on it. She shot back into the room and sat down. I almost fell over her.

He was on the floor, with Madelon Butler under him, groping wildly to get both hands on her throat. She was kicking and beating at his arms, but uttering no sound, while that insane racket kept coming from his open mouth.

I shoved the gun in my belt and hauled him up. He wouldn't turn her loose, and tried to bring her with him. I hit him. He turned his face a little, and finally let her go and looked at me as if he'd never seen me before. I hit him again and felt the pain go up my arm. He was standing there rubber-legged as if he couldn't fall until somebody told him where, so I put my hand in his face and pushed. He stretched out alongside the blonde on the floor. I felt of my hand. It hurt and it had blood on it, but I couldn't feel any broken bones.

Madelon Butler stood up. The dark hair was wild and her eyes were like winter smoke as she came toward me. I didn't know what she was trying to do until I felt the gun sliding out of my belt. I grabbed her wrist, broke her grip on it, and shook her hand off.

"No, you don't," I said. "Sit down."

She didn't seem to hear me, so I shoved her down in the chair at one end of the table. The other two were getting off the floor, and now they both looked crazy. He was crying, and her face was white and her eyes blazed.

I pointed to the chairs at the other end of the table. "You'd better sit down," I said. "I'm tired of wrecking my hands. From now on I use the gun."

His mouth was working. Tears ran down his face. "I'll kill you," he said. "I'll kill you."

"Quiet," I said. I pointed at the chairs again.

They sat down.

I pulled a chair up to the table, halfway between them and Madelon Butler, and sat down myself. I tilted back in the chair a little, put the gun in my lap, and took a cigarette out and lit it.

After all the violence it was suddenly quiet in the room, so still I could hear the sound of my own heavy breathing. Then the blonde's voice came up through it.

Her hands grasped the edge of the table so tightly her fingers were white around the nails. I could see the cords standing out in her throat. Her voice wasn't much more than a whisper that sounded as if it were being pressed out of her by a heavy weight on her chest, but some of the things she said I'd never heard before myself.

It went on and on. Madelon Butler watched her curiously, the way she might study something brought up by a deep-sea trawl. When the blonde finally stopped for breath, she said, "You are a vulgar little gutter rat, aren't you?"

But the blonde was finished. She could only stare silently. She drew her hands across her face and shuddered, and at last she turned to me.

"What are you going to do with her?" she asked.

"Never mind," I said.

"Let me have the gun," she begged. "Just let me have it for five seconds. Let me kill her. I'll give it back to you. You can kill me, or turn me over to the police, but just let me have it."

"Relax," I said. "You'll get ulcers."

"What are you going to do with her?"

Madelon Butler lit a cigarette and watched us through the smoke. The man sat hunched over the other end of the table, holding the edges of it with his hands and saying nothing.

"We're going to take your car and go for a little ride as soon as it's dark. If you don't mind."

"How much is she paying you?"

"Who said she was?" I asked.

"Of course she is. Why else would you do it?"

"I'm her mother."

"How much?"

"Never mind," I said. "I don't think you could meet the price."

She turned her face then and looked at the man. "Didn't you hear him, Jack? You see? The dear, sweet thing couldn't find it. She didn't even know what we were talking about."

"Stop it!" he said.

"She not only double-crossed you then, to get it, but she's using it now to double-cross you again and get away and leave you holding the bag."

"Shut up!"

There was no stopping her. "Why didn't you have sense enough to look? Just look? Did you trust her, or something? Didn't you know what she was? Didn't the other one teach you anything?"

His eyes were terrible. He hit her across the mouth with his open hand. She stopped then, and it became suddenly and almost breathlessly silent in the room. I could even hear the squirrel chattering again, up on the hill.

I looked at my watch. It was only a little after one. We couldn't leave until it was dark. That meant for at least six more hours I had to sit here and keep them sorted out and untangled and away from each other's throats. I had thought that if I got them in here I could turn the gun over to Madelon Butler and let her watch them while I got a little sleep, but I could see that was out. They'd rush her the minute I dropped off. They were crazy enough. Or if they weren't, she'd taunt them into it with that arrogant contempt of hers.

I'd given up trying to figure it out. And there was no use asking any questions. I'd just be wasting my breath. They were all too hell-bent on killing each other to bother with outsiders trying to make sense out of it.

I was tired. It had been thirty hours since I'd had any sleep, and we had a long afternoon and another whole night ahead of us. I wondered what our chances were of getting back to Mount Temple and into that house without being caught. In the dark, and with another car, we shouldn't be stopped on the highway, but the house was another matter. They'd be watching it.

I stood up and motioned toward the storeroom. "In there," I said.

They went by, watching me like a couple of big cats, and walked in. They sat down on some boxes. I stood in the doorway and looked at them.

"You won't get hurt if you stay in there," I said. "And when we leave here you'll be turned loose. But if you try to come back through this door or jump Mrs. Butler again while we're here, you've had it."

"Aren't you brave, with a gun in your hand?" the blonde said.

"Don't keep crowding your luck. Just because I haven't shot you already doesn't mean I won't if I have to. I'm strictly a money player, and there's a lot of it tied up in this. Too much to let a couple of hotheads like you louse it up. Keep it in mind, Blondie."

"I wouldn't count on that money too much," she said.

"You wouldn't? Why?"

"You'll never get it."

"I'll worry about that."

Her eyes had grown thoughtful, and now she actually

smiled. It was a very cold smile. "Yes. You'll worry
about it, before you get through. You haven't found
out yet who you're dealing with. I don't know why I
didn't think of it before, but it makes me feel a lot
better."

"What does?"

"The fact that even if you get away from here, it
really doesn't matter. One of you will kill the other
before it's all over. Isn't it nice?"

"Isn't it?" I said. "Unsaddle your broom and stay a
while."

I closed the door and walked back to the table.

Madelon Butler was still sitting in the chair at the
end of it. I sat down and lit another cigarette.

"You'd better go in and get some sleep," I said.
"You'll need it."

"It's too hot," she said.

"Suit yourself," I said. "But it may be a little hot
tonight, too."

She gave me that supercilious smile of hers again.
"Not afraid to go back there, are you?"

"No," I said. "We're going back."

"You're rather fond of money, aren't you?"

"I don't know," I said. "I never had any."

"I hope you'll be very happy with it."

"I like your friends," I said, nodding toward the
storeroom. "Why don't all of you rent yourselves out to
curdle milk?"

"You're not becoming squeamish, are you?" she
asked mockingly. "Where's your fine, professional attitude? Surely the detached and unemotional Mr. Barton

wouldn't let a little display of petulance like that upset him." She broke off. "By the way, you never did tell me what your name really is."

"That's right," I said. "I didn't, did I?"

She shrugged.

Time dragged. The cabin was stifling.

I dozed off once, propped up in the chair. When my eyes flew open I saw the storeroom door being pulled gently back. The blonde was looking at me. "Back," I said. It shut again.

They'd be watching the house. They might catch us.

Or if we tried to run, it could be worse. They might kill us.

All right. Either I wanted that money, or I didn't.

And if I wanted it, I had to have the keys.

Somehow, the sun went down.

It was dusk out across the clearing. I stood up. Madelon Butler killed another cigarette in the mountain of butts on the tray and looked at me. "Put on your robe," I said. "It's time to go."

"Very well," she said.

I thought of something. "Would that blonde's dress fit you?"

"I haven't the faintest idea. But I'd die before I'd touch it."

"All right," I said. "Don't strip your gears. It doesn't matter. You can change into something else when we get in the house. If we do."

I went over and opened the storeroom door. "All right," I said.

They came out. I motioned for them to go out the

front door. I followed them. Madelon Butler came out, and I handed her the key. "Lock it," I said. She locked the door. I put the key in my pocket.

I nodded to the blonde and Jack. "Just stand right where you are. When we're gone you can start walking. Or you can have that Cadillac if you know how to start it without the keys and don't mind that it's a little hot."

"I'll find you someday," Jack said. "I'll find you."

"I'm in the book," I said. I motioned for Madelon Butler to get into the car.

As we crossed the culvert at the edge of the meadow I tossed the key out at the end of it without slowing down. I looked in the rear-view mirror, but I couldn't see them. It was already too dark under the trees.

I flicked on the headlights and we went up the hill through the timber.

The lights of the country store and filling station were ahead of us. "Here's where we hit the highway," I said. "We'll see a police car once in a while, but they won't be looking for this car. Don't pay any attention to them. They can't see you in here."

"Don't worry about me," she said.

I sailed the keys to the Cadillac into the roadside bushes, and in another minute or two we pulled onto the pavement. In spite of what I'd told her, it was like walking into a cold shower.

I drove carefully, holding it down to forty or forty-five. Just a simple accident or being stopped for a traffic violation of some kind was all it would take to ruin us. I thought of how invisible a car was among all the hundreds of others until something happened to it, or the driver did something wrong, and then it was in the center of the stage with all the spotlights on it. When we came into the first town I turned over one street to keep out of the lights, and went through as if we were driving on eggshells.

I turned twice more, and we were back on the highway again. It was only thirty miles now.

It had been over twelve hours since she was supposed to have fled. They might not actually expect her to be stupid enough to come back, but they'd have at least one man covering the place as a matter of routine. Maybe there'd be more. The money still hadn't been found. They wouldn't be taking any chances.

Would he be in front? Or in back? Inside the house itself?

We had to park the car far enough away so they wouldn't hear it or see the headlights. And still we couldn't walk around on the streets.

"Is there another street or road in back of that one directly behind the house?" I asked.

"Yes," she said. "I'll show you where to turn. There are no street lights there, and it's mostly vacant lots."

She'd grown up in that house. I wondered how she felt about going back to it for the last time and knowing she'd never see it again if we got away. But whatever she felt, she kept it to herself. Then it occurred to me she had never seemed particularly bothered by the fact that her husband wasn't around any more, either, or why he wasn't. She wasn't exactly the gushy type.

"Where did they find him?" I asked.

"I have no idea," she said.

"You don't know?" I asked unbelievingly.

"That's right." She appeared completely uncon-cerned. "You were the one who heard the news report. Remember?"

It just didn't add up. I had to believe her. She sounded as if she were telling the truth, and she had no reason to lie about it now. And she hadn't known that his car had been abandoned right in front of the James girl's apartment, either. An odd thought struck me then. Had she really killed him? But that was stupid. She'd as much as admitted it. She was paying me $120,000 to get her out of there and hide her from the police. For what—a parking ticket?

"You don't make much sense to me," I said.

"Really?" She lit a cigarette, and for an instant the flame of the match lit up the still, intensely beautiful face. "I wasn't aware I was supposed to."

"Did you kill Butler?" I asked.

"Perhaps you should read the terms of our contract again. I recall nothing in it about submitting to an inquisition."

"Have it your way," I said. "I just work here."

"An excellent appraisal of your status. Incidentally, I might say that you have done very well so far, with only one or two exceptions."

"What exceptions?"

"In the first place, you should have killed them instead of turning them loose. They can describe you. And in the second place, you have thrown away the only key I have to the house. It was attached to the car keys."

"We don't need a house key," I said. "We go in through one of the basement windows. And as far as their describing me, you know as well as I do they're not going to the police. They can't."

"Yes. But has it occurred to you they might be *captured* by the police?"

"Sure," I said. "But it's just a chance we have to take."

"Needlessly."

"All right. Needlessly. But I'm doing the job, and I'll do it my own way."

She said nothing. We came up the grade out of the river bottom.

I'd had plenty of warning about her. But I didn't realize it in time.

Chapter Ten

We were nearly there. I could see the glow of lights against the sky.

"Slowly," she said. "We pass a cemetery on the right. And just beyond it there's a road on the left. Turn there."

In a moment I could see the evergreen hedge of the cemetery. Two cars were coming up behind us. I slowed and let them go by.

"Now," she said. "On the left."

I made the turn. It was a gravel road with a field off to the left beyond a fence. We passed a lighted house. A dog ran out and chased us, barking furiously. I cursed, feeling the tension build up inside me.

Coming back here like this with the police after her was insane, and I knew it. Suppose we ran into them? We might get away from them in the dark, but that wasn't the thing. They'd know where we were, and all the roads in this end of the state would be bottled up before we could get out.

But there was nothing else to do. We had to have the keys to get into those boxes. Maybe, under ordinary circumstances, you could have them opened without the keys if you had plenty of time and absolutely foolproof identification. In her case it was utterly impossible. She'd rented them under a phony name, she was a fugitive, and the slightest irregularity or one suspicious move would bring the whole thing down on top of us.

While I was on the subject, I thought of something else.

"Have you got any cash with you?" I asked. "Or at the house, where you can get it?"

"Yes," she said. "I have nearly a thousand dollars in my handbag."

"Good," I said. I didn't ask why she was carrying around that much. It was obvious. She'd known she might have to make a run for it someday, and she was ready.

We turned right and went up a slight grade with trees on both sides of the road. I was driving slowly, drawing a map of it in my mind. We might be in trouble when we came out. There were no houses, no lights. A cat ran across the road, its eyes shining.

"In the next block, where that power line crosses the road," she said.

"Right." I swung the car sharply around, facing back the way we had come, and backed off the road under the overhanging trees. I cut the motor and lights, and we sat still for a moment, letting our eyes become accustomed to the darkness.

We got out, and I gently closed the door. I was conscious of my shallow breathing and the fluttering in my stomach, the way it always was just before the opening kickoff of a football game. The night was overcast and still, the air thick with heat and the smell of dust.

I had changed into the white shirt again back at the

camp, but I had on the coat to cover it. I turned the collar up to hide any gleam of white. The gun and flashlight were in the pockets. I looked at her. She was all right, except for her feet. I could see the faint blur of that white trim around her slippers. It couldn't be helped.

I held her arm for another minute while we listened. There was no sound. "All right," I whispered. "Let's go."

We cut across the lot, following the dark shafts of the power-line poles. There was a path of sorts, and we made no sound. In a minute or two we came out onto the next street, the one directly behind the house. I felt a sidewalk under my feet. There were no cars in sight.

She tugged at my arm. "This way," she whispered. We hurried along the sidewalk, and then cut diagonally across the street. I knew where we were then. I could see the high, shadowy pile of the oleanders. Out the gate, cut left diagonally, half a block, I thought, writing it down in my mind in reverse, the way it would be coming back. I might be in a hurry. And I might be alone.

I eased the gate open, an inch at a time. We slipped through and stood in the dense shadow of the oleanders. I put my lips down next to her ear and whispered.

"Wait here. I want to see if there's a car around anywhere."

She nodded. I could see the faint blur of her face as it moved.

I slipped off across the lawn toward the dark mass

of the house, cutting a little to the right to pass around the south side near the garage. Stopping beside the shrubs near the corner, I searched the driveway. It showed faintly white in the gloom. I could see no car.

Keeping on the grass to muffle any sound, I eased around the side of the house until I could see the front. There was no car here. The night was empty and silent except for the faint sound of music coming from somewhere across the huge expanse of front lawn and the street beyond it. It was a radio in some house on the other side of the street.

I remained motionless for a minute, thinking. They might be parked out on the street, sitting in a car and watching the drive. Or they still might have a man inside. We just had to chance it.

I started back. I came around the rear corner and past the back porch by the kitchen, moving silently on the grass. As I neared the break in the shadowy mass of the oleander hedge where the gate was, I could just make out the little blur of white at her feet. She was moving. She was coming slowly toward the house. I turned a little to meet her, watching the small bits of white fur move across the formless darkness of the lawn. Then they disappeared. They winked off, like a light going out.

I stopped, feeling my heart pound in my throat. She had passed behind something. But there wasn't anything there. There couldn't be. Now I could see them again. She had stopped too. I strained my eyes into the night. I could see nothing at all. Then the blur of white at her feet winked off again. Something was between us, and it was moving.

There was no way to warn her. I wanted to cry out to her to run, but I knew the stupidity of it. The man knew she was there; he could see her feet. But he didn't know I was behind him. I was tense. My mouth was dry.

I could run. I could circle them, get behind them, and make it to the gate and the car.

I didn't run. I couldn't quit now. I started moving toward them, keyed up and scarcely breathing.

Then it happened. She had seen him, or heard him, or somehow sensed that he was there, and thought I was coming back. She whispered, "Here I am." It was like a shout.

Light burst over her face and the upper part of her body. She wasn't twelve feet away, exposed in the glare of the man's flashlight like a floodlighted statue. I was coming up behind him, very fast and as silently as I could, pulling the gun from my pocket, when I heard her gasp. I could see him quite plainly, silhouetted against his own light. I raised the gun and swung.

"All right, Mrs. Butler," he said. "Stand right where you are. You're under ar—"

He grunted, and his arms jerked. The light fell out of his hand as he buckled back against me and then slid to the grass. I lunged for it and snapped it off. Night closed around us again, black as the bottom of a coal mine.

I was scared as I felt for him. Maybe I'd hit him too hard. I located an arm and fumbled at his wrist, trying to feel the pulse, but my hands were shaky and numb and I couldn't tell. I put a hand on his chest. He was breathing normally. The fright began to leave me.

She was leaning over me in the darkness. "I thought it was you," she whispered.

I didn't answer. I was too busy thinking. What did we do with him? He was merely knocked out, and might come around at any time. To go on in the house and leave him lying here would be suicide. She'd have to go alone; I could stay here and watch him. But suppose there was another one inside?

We didn't have all night. Every minute we stayed here made it more dangerous. I had to do something, and fast.

I reached down, took the gun out of his holster, and threw it over into the oleanders. As I did so I heard something rattle. It was metallic, something fastened to his belt. I had the answer then. Running a hand along the belt, I located them and took them off. They were handcuffs.

"Stay where you are," I whispered to her.

Grabbing him by the shoulders, I dragged him across the grass into the deeper shadows under the hedge. I rolled him up against the bottom of a clump of oleanders, pulled his hands behind him, and shackled them together around a couple of the big stems. Then I took his handkerchief out of his pocket, wadded it into his mouth, took off his tie, and made it fast around his head to hold the handkerchief in. He was still out, as limp as a wet shirt. I knelt and listened to his breathing. He was all right.

I hurried back. Leaning close to her, I whispered, "We've got to get out of here fast. You won't have time to change. So just throw some clothes in a bag when we get inside."

She nodded.

I led the way to the window where I'd gone in before. Pulling the screen back, I raised the sash and dropped in; then I helped her. We stood in darkness in the basement, listening. There was no sound except that of our own breathing in the hot, dead air.

"Where are those keys?" I whispered.

"In the kitchen."

"All right. Let's go."

I flicked on the small flashlight and we went up the stairs. I was tense again, and wanting to get out. I felt like a wild animal reaching for the bait in a trap. We stepped into the kitchen, I cut the light, and we listened. There was dead silence. I tiptoed over to the other door and stared through the darkness of the dining room toward the front of the house. I could see only more empty blackness.

I switched on the light again. "Where?" I whispered.

She took my hand and directed the beam. It splashed against one of the white cupboards at the end of the sink, moved slightly again, and came to rest on the end of it. I saw it then. A big ring hung from a nail driven into the wood, a ring filled with a dozen or more of the old, unmarked, and useless keys that a house accumulates in its lifetime—extra car keys, cellar-door keys, trunk keys, front-door keys, and keys to nothing at all. While I stared, she lifted it down.

I held the light for her while she snapped the ring open, slid off three of the keys, and put the others back on the nail. She held the three in the palm of her hand for a moment, looked up at me in the reflected glow of the light with that cool, serene smile of hers, and dropped them into her handbag. I thought of $120,000 hanging there in plain sight among a bunch of discarded and useless junk. She was a smart baby.

The urge to hurry was getting to me again. There could have been two of them out there. One would miss the other, and start looking. Or he might work the gag out of his mouth.

I grabbed her arm and went through the dining room. In the short hallway that led to the stairs I gave her the flashlight. "Make it as fast as you can," I said. "Throw some shoes and a dress in a bag or grab 'em under your arm. Let's get out of here."

I watched her go up the stairs. She turned at the top, and the light was gone. I tried to stand still in the darkness so I could listen, but my feet kept moving. I had the cop's flashlight in my pocket, but didn't take it out. I didn't need a light; all I wanted to do was get out of there.

Why didn't she hurry? She'd been gone a week. What was she doing? Standing in front of a closet full of clothes trying to make up her mind what to wear? Did she think she was going to a dance? I cut it off coldly, forcing myself to realize she'd hardly had time to walk down the hall to her bedroom yet. I waited, shifting from one foot to the other.

Minutes dragged by. At last I saw the beam of light cut through the darkness above me and turn at the head of the stairs. She was coming down. She had a small overnight bag in her hand and had on shoes instead of the fur-trimmed slippers. I grabbed the bag and fell in behind her, hustling her along.

We hurried back through the kitchen and down the

stairs. The heels of her shoes clicked on the concrete floor of the basement. We turned and started toward the window. In another minute we'd be in the open and on our way.

I saw it out of the corner of my eye, and went prickling cold all over. In one motion I grabbed her arm, snatched the flashlight out of her hand, and shut it off. I jammed it in my pocket and put my hand over her mouth before she could even cry out or gasp at the suddenness of it. We remained locked together and suspended in the darkness and I felt her turn her head and look toward the windows. She saw it too. She stiffened.

It was another flashlight, outside. The beam hit the first window. It probed through dirty glass and screen and cobwebs to spatter weakly against the basement wall behind us. She moved a little, and I realized I still had my hand over her mouth. I took it away. The light dropped a little. It hit the floor not five feet away. Then it went out.

I breathed again. Pulling her by the arm, I began backing up. After two or three steps I turned and cut toward where the furnace should be. We had to get behind something. I felt the solid metal of it against my side just as the light snapped on again in front of the second window, the one I had broken. I pulled her quickly after me and we were behind the furnace.

I looked around the edge. Light splashed against the window, steadying up on the place where I had broken the glass. I was squeezing her arm. If it was another cop, he might come in. He'd see the tape and broken glass and realize someone had forced a way in there.

The screen was being drawn back. The window rose.

We couldn't get out. The light was swinging across the basement now, and if we tried to run back he'd see us. Our only chance was to sweat it out, trying to keep the furnace between us and him. The light was pointed down. He dropped in on the concrete floor. He lost his balance and fell. The light dropped and rolled, coming to rest with its beam reflected off the whitewashed wall. I stared. I was looking at high-heeled shoes and a pair of nylon-clad legs that had never belonged to any cop in the world.

She reached for the light and for an instant I saw her face. It was Diana James.

I felt Mrs. Butler start beside me. Then, strangely, she pushed up against me, as if she were scared. She clung to me, gripping my arm. I was too busy to think about it. I didn't know what it was until it was too late.

Diana James was straightening up, reaching for the flashlight. Then, abruptly, Madelon Butler pushed away from me and walked out into the open. I tried to grab her, but it was too unexpected. She picked up the light and shot it right into the other's face.

"Really, Cynthia," she said, "I would have thought you'd have better sense than to come here yourself."

Cynthia? But there wasn't time to wonder about that. The whole thing was like trying to watch the separate stages of an explosion and knowing all you were ever going to see was the end result and that all in one piece. Diana James straightened in the merciless glare of the light, her eyes going bigger and bigger in terror. Her mouth tried to form something, but just opened and stayed there.

It was at exactly this moment that I felt the lightened weight of my coat and knew why she had pressed up against me in the dark. I lunged for her, still knowing there was nothing I could do, that I was just trying to catch pieces of something that was happening all at once.

She shot. The gun crashed. It roared and reverberated back and forth across the concrete-walled sound chamber of a basement where I'd been afraid of the tapping of her heels against the floor. Before I could grab her, she shot again, the sound swelling and exploding against my eardrums with almost physical pain. In all this madness of noise I saw Diana James jerk around, one hand going up to her chest, and then spill forward onto the floor like a collapsing column of children's blocks. Just as I reached Madelon Butler and got my hands on her, the light tilted downward and splashed across the fallen dark head and the grotesque swirl of skirt and long legs and arms already still.

Silence rolled back and fell in on us. It was like a vacuum. I could hear it roaring in my ears. I grabbed her. "*You—*" I said. But there were no words. Nothing would come out. I had an odd feeling I was merely standing there to one side watching myself go crazy. I tried to shove her toward the window.

"Here's your gun," she said calmly.

I didn't even know why I took it. I threw it, and heard the clatter as it hit a wall and fell to the floor.

"Get out that window!"

But she was gone. The flashlight snapped off and I was in total darkness, alone. I swept my arms around madly and felt nothing. Somehow I remembered the other flashlights in my pocket. I clawed one out and started to switch it on, but some remnant of sanity stopped me just in time. We had less than one chance in a thousand of getting out of there now before the whole town fell in on us, and we wouldn't have that if we showed any light.

I started groping toward where the window should be. Maybe she was already there. Light flared behind me. I whirled. "Turn that out!" I lashed at her. Then I saw what she was doing. It was the ultimate madness.

It wasn't the flashlight. She had struck a match and was setting fire to the mountainous pile of old papers and magazines beside the coal bin. An unfolded paper burst into flame. I leaped toward her. She grabbed up another and spread it open with a swing of her arm, dropping it on the first. I slammed into her and beat at the flames. It was hopeless.

Another caught. The fire mounted, throwing flickering light back into the corners of the basement and beginning to curl around the wooden beams above us. I fell back from it.

"Run!" I shouted.

She went toward the window. I pounded after her. I stumbled over something. It was the small traveling case I had set down. Without knowing why, I grabbed it up as I bounced back to my feet and lunged after her. I boosted her out the window. I threw the bag out. Then I knelt beside Diana James. I touched her throat, and knew it made no difference now whether we left her there or not. She was dead.

We ran across the black gulf of the lawn. The night

was still silent, as if the peace of it had never been broken by the sound of shots. At the gate I looked back once. The basement windows were beginning to glow. In a few minutes the house would be a red mountain of flame.

Chapter Eleven

We shot out the gate and across the pavement. As we plunged into the path by the power line I heard a siren behind us, somewhere in town. Somebody had reported the shots.

I could hear her laboring for breath, trying to keep up. She stumbled in the dark and I yanked her up savagely by her arm. I wished she were dead. I wished she'd never been born, or that I had never heard of her. She had wrecked it all. I didn't even know any more why I was dragging her with me. Maybe it was pure reflex.

I had the keys out of my pocket before we reached the dense shadow under the trees where we'd left the car. I threw the bag in and began to punch the starter while she was running around to the other side and climbing in. The ceiling light flicked on and then off again as both doors closed, and in that short instant of time and in all the madness some part of my mind was still clear enough to grasp the awful thing I hadn't noticed until now, until it was too late.

She didn't have her purse.

Her hands were empty. She had left the purse back there in the house. Tires screamed as we shot ahead down the hill. I ground on the throttle, peering ahead into the lights for the turn that would come flying back at us. *She didn't have the purse.* I saw the turn just in time. We slammed into it and threw gravel over into the field as we skidded around, and then we were straightened out again.

The highway was coming up now. No cars were in sight. We hurtled onto it, headed south. I was raging.

She'd killed Diana James and brought the cops down on us. All the roads would be blocked inside of an hour. And the big, final, most horrible joke of all was that the thing I had been after all the time, the thing that had got me into this, was gone. I thought of those three keys fire-blackened and lost forever in the ashes of the house. Even the thousand dollars in cash was gone. We had nothing. We were wanted by all the police in the country, and didn't have enough money to hide ourselves for a week.

She took a cigarette out of the breast pocket of the robe and lit it, and leaned back in the seat. "You appear to be unhappy about something," she said.

"You little fool!"

"Didn't you appreciate the funeral pyre for your charming friend?" she asked calmly. "I thought it rather a nice touch. Something Wagnerian about it."

"You stupid—"

I choked. It was no use. It was beyond me. I could only watch the highway flying back at us in the night. And watch the rear-view mirror for cars behind us. Where would they try to block us? Beyond that next town? Or before?

"You *are* provoked, aren't you?"

I found the words at last. "Don't you realize yet what you've done?" I raged at her. "You might as well have called them on the phone and told 'em where we were. We've got about a chance in a million of getting away. And on top of that, you went off and left the thing we came back for."

"Oh," she said easily. "I see now what's bothering you. You mean the keys?"

"Where did you leave the purse? Not that it matters now."

"I didn't leave it," she said. "It's in that bag."

I felt suddenly weak. Then I remembered that the only reason I had picked the bag up back there in the basement in all that confusion had been the fact that I'd stumbled over it. I felt even weaker. It was nearly a minute before I could even talk.

"All right. But look. By this time your whole lawn is full of cops. They've got radio cars. And there are only four highways out of Mount Temple. They're all going to be plugged. We may not get past the next town."

"Quite right," she said. "We don't even go to the next town. About six miles ahead, just before you go down into that river bottom, a dirt road turns off to the right. It runs west about ten miles and crosses another country road going south."

"How far south can we get on it?"

"I'm not sure. But there are a number of them, and by switching back and forth we should be able to go over a hundred miles before we have to come back on a highway. And they can't watch them all."

It was our only chance, and it might work. I could feel the beginnings of hope. And at the same time I was conscious of a terrible yearning to get off that highway before it was too late. The six miles were a thousand. I rode on the throttle. We blasted on into the tunnel the lights made. We came around a long curve and I saw the taillights of a car far ahead. I slowed a little, hating it. We couldn't pass anybody at that speed. It might be a cruising cop.

Minutes dragged by while we crawled along at fifty-five. "We're getting near," she said. I slowed, watching the mirror. Another car was behind us, but it was far back. We swung around another curve, and I saw the signboard. Nobody was in sight when we made the turn. I sighed with relief. The tension was off, for a while, anyway.

Then it rolled up from behind and caught me, the instant I relaxed. The tension wasn't off. And maybe it never would be.

She had pulled the trigger, but I was in as deep as she was. I'd been there, it was the gun I was carrying, and I had helped her to escape. And if they ever caught us, it'd just be my word against hers. That was nice, wasn't it? A jury would take one look at the two of us, and hang me without going out of the room. I felt sick.

It was a narrow gravel road, very rough and full of right-angled turns going around cotton fields. After a mile or two we went up over a slight rise and plunged into a dense forest of pine. There were no houses, no lights anywhere. I stopped.

"You drive," I said. I got out and went around to the other side while she slid under the wheel.

"What are you going to do?" she asked.

"Look at the map. If I can find one."

She started up. I took the flashlight out of my

pocket and pawed through the usual collection of junk in the glove compartment. Down at the bottom I found a state highway map. I unfolded it.

Here was Mount Temple. Two hundred miles south, on the Gulf, was Sanport. I ran my finger along the main north-south highway and found the faint line that was the unnumbered secondary road we were on. It went on and came out on another north-south highway about forty miles west. But I could see, just ahead of where we should be now, the intersecting road she had mentioned. It ran south for about thirty miles before it ended on another east-west secondary road. We could shift west on that one for about fifteen miles and we'd hit another going south. I traced on through the maze of faint lines. It could be done. We could get down through that back country for nearly 150 miles before coming back on a main highway again, and when we did, we'd have a choice of at least three roads converging on the city. They couldn't cover all of them.

Gasoline?

I shot a glance at the gauge. It was a little over half full. It might be enough. But this would be poor country to try to cut it fine. I looked back at the map. About seventy-five miles south we'd go through a small town. We could fill up there.

I lit a cigarette and glanced around at her. The soft glow of the dash lights was on her face. I studied it for a moment while she rammed the car ahead between the dark walls of pine. What kind of woman was this, anyway? It hadn't been thirty minutes since she had killed another woman, she had probably murdered her husband, she had burned down that enormous house she had lived in all her life, she was running from the police, and yet she could have been merely driving over to a neighbor's to play bridge for all the emotion she showed.

But still it wasn't in any way an expressionless doll's face. It was just intensely proud and self-contained. Maybe she felt things and maybe she didn't; but win, lose, or draw, it was her business. She didn't advertise. There was a cool and disdainful sort of arrogance about it that didn't give a damn for what anybody thought—or for anybody, for that matter.

At least that made us even on that. I didn't care much for her either.

"Not so worried now?" she asked. I could hear the faint undertone of contempt.

"Look, Hard Stuff," I said. "I'll make out all right. Don't fret about it. It's just that if you're trying to hide from the police, I don't see any sense in telling them where you are by killing people just for laughs. Or starting a bonfire to attract attention. So let's don't try it again. You might get hurt yourself."

"Careful," she said mockingly. "Remember how much I'm worth to you alive."

"What do you think I've been remembering? The touch of your hand?"

"Quite proud of your tough attitude, aren't you?"

"It's a tough world."

She said nothing. In a few minutes we hit the cross-road. She turned left. The road began to drop a little toward the river country. It was wild and sparsely settled, and we met no cars.

"See if you can find a place to get off the road," I said. "You've got to change those clothes."

"All right."

She slowed. In a few minutes we saw a pair of ruts leading off into the timber. She pulled off far enough to be out of sight of the road, and stopped in a small open space where there was room to turn around.

I got out, but before I did I lifted the keys out of the ignition. She saw it. She smiled. "Trust me, don't you?"

"You think I'm stupid?" I gestured toward the traveling bag. "Change in the car. And let me know when you're ready to go."

I walked back a short distance toward the road and lit a cigarette. The sky was still overcast, and night pressed down over the river bottom with an impenetrable blackness and a silence that seemed to ring in my ears. Nothing moved here. We were alone.

Alone?

They were drawing circles around us on the map. The radio was snapping orders, efficient and coded and deadly. Police cars raced down highways in the darkness all around us. Like hell we were alone. We had lots of company; it was just spread out around us, waiting.

I turned my head and I could see the red glow of the car's taillights behind me. We could beat them. They had everything in their favor except the two things they had to have to win: a description of the car and a description of me. They didn't know who I was or what I looked like, or even that I existed. If I could keep them from seeing her, we could make it.

I finished the cigarette and flipped it outward in the

darkness. She called softly. I turned. She had opened one of the car doors so the ceiling light would come on. When I walked up, she was holding a mirror and putting lipstick on her mouth.

She had changed into a skirt and a dark blouse about the color of her eyes. The sleeves of the blouse were full and then tight-fitting about the wrists, and below them her hands were slender and pale and very beautiful. She finished with the lipstick, put the mirror back in her purse, and looked up at me.

"How do I look?" she asked.

"Fine," I said. "For a woman who's just murdered another one, you look great."

"You have a deplorable command of English," she said. "Don't you find murdered a bit pretentious as applied to vermin? Why not exterminated? Or simply removed?"

"Yes, Your Highness. Excuse me for breathing. Now, take those three keys out of your purse and hand them here."

"Why?"

"Because I like your company. I adore you, and wouldn't have you leave me for anything."

"They're no good to you alone."

"I know. But they are to you. And if we get clear of here tonight you might suddenly decide you didn't need any more help—not at today's prices. I can't watch you all the time. I have to sleep occasionally, and I don't intend to follow you to the john. So just to remove the temptation, I'll take charge of them."

Her eyes met mine coolly, not quite defying me, but just testing me and watching.

"There's an easy way," I said, "and a hard way. How do you want it?"

She took the three keys out of her purse and put them in my hand.

"That's better," I said. I put them in my wallet.

I looked at my watch. It was nine-twenty. I could feel that awful urge to run and run faster and keep on running take hold of me again. I got behind the wheel and we rolled back on the road. We shot ahead in the darkness.

We crossed the river on a long wooden bridge. The road began to rise again. We couldn't make much speed. There were too many chuckholes in the road. I managed to keep it around forty.

"Just where, precisely, are we going?" she asked.

"Sanport. Thirty-eight-twenty-seven Davy Avenue. Memorize it, in case we get separated. My apartment's on the third floor. Number Three-o-three."

"Number Three-o-three. Thirty-eight-twenty-seven Davy," she repeated. "That's easy to remember."

"And my name's Scarborough. Lee Scarborough."

"Is that authentic? Or another alias?"

"It's my right name."

"To what do I owe this unprecented confidence? You wouldn't tell me before."

"With those two people listening? You think I'm crazy?"

"Oh," she said. "And, in case we do get to Sanport alive, what do we do with the car?"

"I'm going to take it to the airport and ditch it. After I get you into the apartment. I'll take a taxi or limousine back to town."

"That's a little obvious," she pointed out. "I mean, if we were really taking a plane, we'd leave the car anywhere but at the airport."

"I know. But they'll never be sure. As a matter of fact, they may never get a lead on this car, anyway. But even if they do, and find it out there, all they can do is suspect you're in Sanport. You'll be on ice. You'll never go out on the street."

"We can't get the money out of the vaults unless I go out."

"I know. But we can wait until some of the heat's off. How long is the rent paid on them?"

"For a year. A year from July, that is."

"All right. It's easy, if we just get there. You stay right in the apartment for at least a month. Maybe longer. We do what we can to change your appearance. I'm working on that now. Maybe we'll make you a redhead. Change you from the skin out, cheap, flashy clothes, that sort of thing. There's only one thing, though. How many times have you been in that bank where you rented the boxes?"

"Banks," she said. "They're in three different ones. I was in each of them only once."

"Well, it's all right, then. They won't remember what you looked like. If you've changed from a brunette to a redhead, they'll never notice. I understand it's been done before, anyway."

"So if I don't go mad in a month of being shut up in that apartment, and I manage to get the money out without being recognized, what then? You murder me, I suppose, and leave the country? Is that it?"

"I've already told you," I said. "I take you to the

Coast. San Francisco, for instance. In my car. I could buy a trailer and let you ride in that, out of sight, but I don't think it'll be necessary if your appearance can be changed enough. You can take out a Social Security card under the name of Susie Mumble or something and go to work. They'll never get you—if you lay off the juice and keep your mouth shut."

"Go to work as a waitress, I suppose?"

"Waitress. Carhop. B-girl. Who cares? As a matter of fact, with your looks you'd never have to work anywhere very long."

"Well, thank *you*. Do you mean my looks as they are now, or after I've suffered a month of your remodeling?"

I shrugged. "Either way. You'd come out a beautiful wench no matter what we did. There'd be plenty of wolves drooling to support you."

"I like your objective appraisal. I take it you don't include yourself among them?"

"You're a business proposition to me, a hundred and twenty thousand dollars' worth of meat to deliver on the hoof. I like my women warm to the touch. And not quite so deadly with a gun."

"I am already aware of the vulgar depths of your taste. Diana James, for instance."

I saw Diana James turn a little, as if someone had twitched at her clothing, and collapse, sprawling on the concrete floor.

"Why did you call her Cynthia?" I asked, remembering.

"Because that was her real name. Cynthia Cannon."

"Why did she change it?"

"Why does any criminal?"

"I thought she was a nurse."

"I believe she was."

I shrugged. "All right. It's nothing to me. I don't give a damn. I don't care how you killed Butler, why you killed him, or where, or who helped you. I don't care who those two blonds were, or how they got in it, or why they wanted to kill you. I don't care why you shot Diana James, or whatever her name was, or why she changed her name."

"Well, that's good," she said.

"Shut up till I finish. There's just one thing I care about, and you'd better be telling the truth about that. If there's not any hundred and twenty thousand in those three boxes, or you try to run out with it, hell will never hold you."

"Don't worry. It's there."

"Baby," I said, "it had better be."

Chapter Twelve

We tried the radio.

It crooned, and gave away thousands of dollars, and told jokes cleaned up with kissing, and groaned as private eyes were hit on the head, and poured sirup on us, and after a long time there was some news. Big Three, it said, and investigation, and tax cut, and budget, and Senator Frammis in a statement this morning, but nothing about Butler.

It was too soon.

We were pounding over a rough road in a vacuum of dead silence and blackness while all around us the sirens were screaming and teletypes were chattering and police cars were taking stations on highways intersecting a circle they had drawn on the map like a proposition in plane geometry, but it was too soon for anybody to know about it except the hunters and the hunted.

I cursed and turned the radio off.

She lit a cigarette and leaned back in the seat. "Don't be so intense, Mr. Scarborough," she said with amusement. "We'll get through. Cyclops is feeling only the backs of the sheep."

"What?"

"Never mind. I guess they haven't made a comic book of it yet."

"Go choke yourself," I said.

"A month. One whole, enchanting month."

"Don't worry. If I can stand it for a hundred and twenty grand, you should be able to put up with it to stay out of the electric chair."

"It would seem so, wouldn't it?"

I shrugged her off and concentrated on driving. We came out at last on the intersecting east-west road and turned right, watching for the one that crossed going south. I looked at the time. It was nearly eleven. The few farmhouses we passed were dark. I began to watch the gasoline gauge. It was dropping faster than I had expected. It must be nearly thirty miles to that small town on the map. And if we got there too late, everything might be closed.

It was a race between the gas gauge and the clock. When we saw the lights of the little town ahead it was ten minutes till midnight and the gauge had been on empty for two miles.

"Get down out of sight while we go through," I said.

"Aren't we going to get gasoline?" she asked.

"Not with you in the car."

She got down, squatting on the floor with her head and shoulders on the seat. I drove through without stopping, looking for an open gas station and knowing that if we didn't find one we were sunk. It was a one-street town two blocks long, with half a dozen cars parked in the puddle of light in front of the lone café. There was a garage at the end of the street, on a corner.

It was open.

The attendant in white coveralls stood in the empty drive between the pumps and watched us go past. I'd been afraid of that. But it couldn't be helped. Anything moving at all in a town like this would be seen.

I drove on, past the scattered dark houses at the edge of town, hoping there would be enough left in the tank to get back. We went around a curve and the lights were gone, swallowed up in the night behind us. I slowed. We crossed a wooden bridge where willows grew out over the roadside ditch. I slid to a stop.

"Wait right here," I said. "I'll be back in a few minutes. And don't show yourself on the road until you're sure it's me. I'll flip the lights up and down before I stop."

"All right," she said. She got out of the car.

There were no cars in sight. I made a fast U turn and headed back.

I stopped in the pool of light in the driveway. The attendant came over. He was a big black-headed kid with a grin. "Fill 'er up?" he asked, looking at me with faint curiosity. He knew it was the same car he'd just seen going past headed south.

"Yeah," I said. "It's empty. Just lucky I noticed it before I got clear out of town."

He shoved the nozzle in the tank. It was the automatic type that shuts itself off. He went around in front and checked the oil and water and started cleaning the windshield while the bell on the pump tinkled away the gallons. I could hear a radio yammering in the office. It sounded funny, like a cab dispatcher's radio, cutting off, coming on, going off again. I couldn't tell what it was saying.

The kid jerked his head toward the car's license tags

and said, "Lot of excitement up your way tonight."

I could feel my mouth dry up. "How's that?"

"Mrs. Butler again. You don't happen to know her, do you?"

"No," I said. "Why?"

"Just thought maybe you did, seeing as you're from the same county. She's got this whole end of the state in an uproar. With all the cops looking for her, she comes right back to her own house. Or at least they figure it must have been her. Some man with her, too, from the looks of it. They slugged a deputy sheriff and shackled him with his own handcuffs, and the house got afire some way."

"All this on the radio?" I asked. "I didn't hear anything about it."

He grinned. "You might say on the radio." He jerked his head toward the office. "Police bands. Not supposed to have it, but back here off the highway they don't say anything. Boy, the air's really burnin' tonight."

"You say there's a man with her?" I asked.

"Almost has to be, the way they figure it. Somebody slugged that deputy so hard he may not live. Broken skull. He's still unconscious."

I turned my face away in the pool of light and cupped my hands as I lit a cigarette. "That's too bad," I said.

"Yeah. They're just hoping he comes out of it. Maybe he'll be able to tell 'em what happened. Somebody said they heard shots, too."

"Sounds like a wild night," I said.

"They'll catch 'em. They're stopping everything on

the highways. Roadblocks. Course, they don't know what the man looks like, but they got a good description of her. They say she's a dish. A real pin-up. You ever see her?"

"Not that I know of," I said.

"I thought maybe, being from the same county—"

If he said that once more, my head would blow up like a hand grenade. "I don't belong to the country club set," I said. "I run a one-lung sawmill, and the only time I ever see any bankers is when they tell me my notes are overdue. How much I owe you?"

"Four-sixty," he said.

I took a five out of my wallet, feeling the wonderful, hard outlines of the three keys through the leather. They were something you could touch. They were no dream you were chasing; you had them in your hand and could feel them.

A man lying unconscious somewhere with a broken skull—a man you didn't know and had never seen except as a block of shadow a little darker than the night—didn't really exist as long as you didn't think about him. I felt the keys through the limp leather.

I thought of the café up the street. I hadn't eaten anything for thirty-six hours; I was dead on my feet and needed coffee to keep going. I heard the cash register ring in the office, and then the radio cut in again with some coded signal that was like a finger pointing. There he is, it seemed to say.

He's standing there in the night. We're in the dark, watching him.

Eat?

Run. Keep going.

Nobody could eat with them looking at his back. When we were safe in the apartment, that feeling of always being watched from behind would go away. Wouldn't it?

Sure it would.

A car rolled in off the street and stopped on the other side of the pumps, and when I turned and looked at it I saw the state seal on the front door of a black Ford sedan and a man getting out dressed in gray whipcord with a Sam Browne belt and a gun holster with a flap on it. I looked at him and then slowly turned my head and stared out into the street, feeling exposed and skinless in the hot pool of light.

"Hey, Sammy," he said, "how about a little service?"

Sammy came out of the office with my change. He grinned at the cop and said, "Boom-de-boom-*boom*. Keep your shirt on, Sergeant Friday."

He handed me the change, and I had to turn to take it. I saw the cop come between the pumps and stand in front of the car, the impersonal face and the gray impersonal eyes turned toward me and toward it, gathering us up in that efficient, remorseless, and completely automatic glance that knew instantly and without conscious thought all there was to know about the outside of both of us, sifting the information, cataloguing it, and storing it away in the precise pigeonholes of his mind, all of this in one instant and without ever breaking off his good-natured kidding of Sammy.

He knew the car was from Madelon Butler's county. The license plates would tell him that automatically. I saw him walk down the side of the car, still talking to

Sammy, and glance carelessly in the windows, front and back. It was all right. He wouldn't see anything. There wasn't anything in the car except that small bag, which could be mine.

I remembered then, but there was nothing I could do except stand there and wait in an agony of suspense.

She had changed clothes in the car. What had she done with the pajamas and the robe? They were either in the bag or on the back seat in plain sight. I didn't know. And I couldn't see in from here.

He came on past the car, glanced idly at me once more, and went over to the Coke machine by the door.

I walked on rubbery legs around to the other side of the car, and as I got in I managed to shoot a glance into the back. There was nothing in sight. She had put them in the bag. I was weak with relief.

"Come back again," Sammy said.

"You bet."

I drove off, feeling him there behind me. It was as if I had eyes in the middle of my back.

I held the speed down while the lights faded behind me. They disappeared as I swung around the curve. I could see the bridge coming up. There were no other cars in sight, ahead or behind. I flipped the lights up on high beam and then down, and hit the brakes.

She came up quickly out of the shadows and climbed in. I shot the car ahead while she was closing the door. The speedometer climbed. We were away. Maybe we would make it. We were only a little over a hundred miles from Sanport now and steadily slipping farther through their fingers.

But behind us Diana James was dead. And if that

deputy sheriff died of his fractured skull, I was a cop killer. Maybe you never could get far enough away from that. There might not be that much distance in the world.

We were almost there. Traffic lights were flashing amber along the boulevard. I looked at my watch. It was a quarter of three. I turned right on a crosstown artery before we got into the business district and went out toward the beach. It was hot and still, and I could feel the stickiness of high humidity. There were few cars on the streets. Newspaper trucks rumbled past, dropping piles of papers on corners.

There wasn't time to pick one up now. The thing I had to do first was get her out of sight once and for all and ditch this car. Then I could relax.

"It's only a few blocks more," I said.

"That's good," she replied. "I'm tired. And I need a drink. You do have something there, I hope?"

"Yes. But remember what I told you about the juice."

"Oh," she said impatiently, "don't be an idiot."

I turned left into a wide, palm-lined avenue. The apartment building was two blocks up. I slowed as we neared it, looking in through the wide glass doors. The foyer was deserted. There was slight chance we would meet anyone at this time in the morning.

I had to go on nearly another block to find a place to park. We got out. The street was quiet. I took the bag.

"If we meet anybody," I said, "just don't let him get a good look at your face. Be looking in your purse or something. There are a hundred apartments in the building. Nobody knows more than half a dozen of the other people. Just act natural."

"Of course," she said. She was completely unconcerned.

We walked down to the doors, our heels clicking on the pavement. The foyer was empty, the doors of the self-service elevator open. We stepped in and I punched the button. When we got out on the third floor the corridor was deserted and silent. Our feet made no sound on the carpet. Number 303 was the second door. I took the key out of my pocket. The door opened silently and we went in.

I closed it very gently, and when it latched I could feel the tension draining out of me. We were safe now. We were invisible. That snarling and deadly hornet swarm of police was locked away on the other side of the door.

I flicked the wall switch. A shaded table lamp came on. The Venetian blinds were tightly closed. She looked around the living room as casually as visiting royalty inspecting the accommodations and then turned to me and smiled.

"Sanctuary," she said, "in Grand Rapids modern. And now could I have a drink?"

"Is that all you've got to say?"

She shrugged. "If you insist. I'm very glad we got here. You were quite effective, Mr. Scarborough. Expensive, but effective."

"Thank you, Your Highness. Don't you ever worry about your neck at all?"

She stopped her inspection of the room to look at me, the large eyes devoid of any expression whatever. "Not publicly," she said. Then she added, "I'll take bourbon and plain water."

If she wanted ice water, I thought, all she had to do was open a vein.

I nodded my head toward the doorway at the left of the living room. "Bath is in that hallway," I said. "The bedroom is just beyond. Dining room and kitchen to the right."

She raised her eyebrows. "*The* bedroom? Where are you going to sleep?"

She was running true to form, all right. I'd intended to turn the bedroom over to her, but she had already taken it for granted. The help could rustle up its own quarters.

"Oh," I said, "I'll just bed down on an old sweater outside your door and bark if I hear burglars."

"You are clever," she murmured. "You don't mind, do you? I just wanted the situation clarified."

"It is clarified. I won't bother you. This is strictly business with me. You're probably frigid, anyway. Aren't you?"

The eyes were completely blank. "No ice," she said. "What?"

"The drink, dear. Remember?"

I went into the kitchen and got the bottle out of the cupboard. I mixed two drinks, making mine very short and weak. While I was out there I looked in the refrigerator to see if there was anything to eat. There was only an old piece of cheese. I could get something at the airport. But what about her?

The hell with her.

I took the drinks in. She was sitting on the sofa with her legs crossed and the dark skirt pulled down over her knees. She had long, lovely legs.

I took a sip of my drink and looked at my watch. I'd have to hurry and ditch that car so I could get back here before people were astir.

Something had been puzzling me, however, and I thought about it now. "Why do you suppose Diana James went up there?" I asked.

"It's fairly obvious," she said. "She had all your rapacious greediness for money. She read—or heard over the radio—that I had fled the country, and she was just hoping I hadn't had time to pick it up when I ran. A sort of desperation try, you might call it."

"I suppose so," I said. "But why did you shoot her? Or do you ever need any particular reason?"

"I shot her because she set foot in my house," she said simply. "She knew I would, of course, but she thought I was gone."

I remembered the awful horror in her eyes when that light burst on her and she heard Madelon Butler call her Cynthia. She had known she was dead when she heard it.

"Why did you start that fire?"

"The house was mine," she said coldly. "It belonged to my grandfather and my father, and I'm the only one of the family left alive. I'm sure no one can question my right to burn it."

"Except the insurance company."

"Why?" she asked calmly. "They'll never have to pay. There is no one to pay it to."

I thought of that. She was right. She no longer existed as Madelon Butler.

I was right, too; but I didn't know the half of it.

Chapter Thirteen

It was fifteen miles out to the airport. The drink propped me up for a few minutes, but when it wore off I was more dead on my feet than ever. I wondered if I had ever slept. There was no traffic, however, and it didn't take long.

I drove into the parking area. It was dark and no one was around. Before I got out I rubbed my handkerchief over the steering wheel and dash and the cigarette lighter. I left the keys in the ignition, and as I got out I smeared the door handle with the palm of my hand.

It would do. There was very little chance they'd ever connect us with this car. That blonde and her brother were in no position to report it. They'd keep their mouths shut. The car might eventually be stolen, with the keys left in it, and God knew where it would wind up. And even if the police did get on the trail of it and find it out here, they'd never know for sure whether we'd left it here as a blind or whether we'd actually taken a plane.

I walked back down the rows of cars and went into the main building. A few people waited for planes. The loud-speaker system was calling somebody's name: Please come to the American Airlines desk. I looked at the clock. It was five minutes of four. I had plenty of time.

The morning papers were on the stand. I reached for one, and she jumped right in my face. There was her picture spread over two columns of the front page, looking as beautiful and arrogant as life.

"SOUGHT!" the caption said.

I dropped a nickel in the cup and folded the paper over as if I had to hide her while I hurried into the coffee shop. I sat down alone at the end of the counter and said, "Hotcakes and coffee," to the waitress without even seeing her.

So she was sought. I knew that. What about that deputy sheriff?

I unfolded the paper and put it on the counter beside me, in such a hurry to read it all that even the headlines blurred. Somebody was saying something.

I looked up. The waitress was still there.

"What?"

"I said did you want your coffee now?"

"Yes."

She was gone. I looked back at the paper, furiously scanning the headlines. It was under her picture.

"OFFICER'S CONDITION CRITICAL," it said.

He wasn't dead.

But that was hours ago.

Carl L. Madden, 29, deputy sheriff of Vale County, is in serious condition in a Mount Temple hospital following an attack by an unknown assailant last night.

    Madden, who has not regained consciousness following the brutal slugging, was on duty at the time as one of the officers maintaining a round-the-clock watch on the home of the late J. N. Butler at the edge of town.

As a result of the sudden eruption of violence and confusion that followed, during which the old Butler mansion burned to the ground, Madden was not discovered until nearly an hour after the attack. Police were first alerted by telephone calls from residents in the vicinity of the Butler place, who reported having heard gunshots. A patrol car was dispatched to the scene.

Upon entering the grounds, the officers discovered the whole basement area of the house in flames. A hurried call brought firemen to the scene, but the fire had gained too much headway and could not be brought under control.

The absence of Madden was noted shortly by other officers who were aware he had been assigned to keep the home under surveillance against the possible return of Mrs. Butler. This, coupled with the reports of gunshots, led to a horrified belief he might be inside the building, perhaps badly injured. An attempt was made to gain entry and institute a search, but was repulsed almost immediately as mounting walls of flame engulfed the old, tinder-dry house.

As the flames lit up the surrounding area, however, he was discovered unconscious and shackled with his own handcuffs to the base of some oleanders at the rear of the grounds. Taken immediately to a hospital, he was described by physicians as suffering from severe concussion and possible fracture of the skull.

*He had apparently been hit from behind with
great force with some hard object, such as a piece of
pipe or a gun. No weapon was found.*

*Local officers are inclined to rule out the possi-
bility that Madden could have been slugged by Mrs.
Butler herself. They state that from the force of the
blow it was almost certainly delivered by a man,
and a big and perhaps powerful one, at that. They
do believe, however, that Mrs. Butler was involved,
and the state-wide search for her has been intensi-
fied. She is already wanted in connection with the
murder of her husband.*

*An instant alarm was sounded, and all highways
leading out of Mount Temple have been under constant patrol since minutes after the fire was discovered. It is considered extremely improbable that she
could have slipped through the police cordon....*

I looked up. "What?"

It was the waitress again. "Here's your coffee."

"Oh," I said. "Thanks."

"They publish those papers ever' day," she said,
"That the first one you ever saw?"

"I just got back from South America."

"Oh." She glanced at the paper. "Pretty, isn't she?"

"Who?"

"Mrs. Butler. That's her picture. She killed her
husband and threw him in an old well. What do you
suppose made her do it?"

I wished she would go away. "Maybe he snored,"
I said.

It was nice. I'd been tied to Mrs. Butler like a

Siamese twin for over twenty-four hours, but a waitress in an airport greasy-spoon had to tell me where they'd found her husband's body.

"No," the waitress went on, answering her own question, "I'll tell you. He was triflin' on her. That's the way it always is. A woman kills her husband, it's because he was tomcattin' around. You men are all triflers."

"All right," I said. "I'll shoot myself. But could I have the hotcakes first?"

She went away. Maybe she would break a leg, or forget to come back. I jerked my eyes back to the paper, feverishly looking for the place where I'd been interrupted. I found it. It was at the bottom of the page. "See Butler, page four," it said.

I flipped the pages, goaded with impatience. I overshot page four and had to back up. Here it was.

No theory has been advanced as to why the house was set afire. A landmark in the county since the early 1890's, it was totally destroyed. Only a chimney and a portion of one wall remained at an early hour this morning.

Police are also at a loss to explain the shots heard by neighbors. Madden's gun, found nearby, had not been fired. A constant vigil is being maintained at his bedside in the hope that a return to consciousness may clear up some of the deep pall of mystery that hangs over the whole affair. It is hoped he may have seen his assailant before he was slugged.

Mrs. Butler has been sought by police since the discovery of the body of her husband, vice-president of the First National Bank of Mount

Temple, in an abandoned well near their summer camp on Crystal Springs Lake, 15 miles east of Mount Temple. Police, acting on a tip by two small boys, discovered the body of the missing banker a little over twenty-four hours ago, ending a nation-wide search that began June 8, when he disap-peared, allegedly absconding with $120,000 of the bank's funds.

No trace of the money was found with the body.

I closed the paper. The waitress brought the hot-cakes and said something I didn't catch. She went away. I forgot the hotcakes.

He was still alive four hours ago. No, it was less than that. The story had said "at an early hour this morning." He would live. He had to. He was young, wasn't he? Twenty-nine was young enough to take a thing like a broken skull.

It hadn't been real before, when I'd heard about it from the filling-station boy. It was only a rumor. But there was something about seeing it in print that made it true.

I tried to sort out how I felt. There wasn't any feeling about the man himself. I didn't know him. I'd never seen him. If he walked up and sat down beside me at the counter here right now I wouldn't know him. He was completely faceless, like a thousand other people that died every day. You read about them. They were killed in automobile wrecks and they fell in bath-tubs and broke their necks and they died of cancer and they fell off buildings and you read about them and then you turned the page and read the funnies.

That wasn't it.

It was that if he died, this wasn't a game I could quit when I got the money. I'd never be able to quit.

This thing was like a swamp. Every time you moved, you sank into it a little deeper. I remembered how simple it had been at first. All I had to do was search an empty house. If I found the money, I was rich. If I didn't, I was out two days' work. That was all. It didn't cost anything.

"There'll be no wild-haired babes blowing their tops and killing each other in anything I'm mixed up in," I had told Diana James. It was a business proposition.

And now Diana James was dead. And a cop was in the hospital with a broken skull. If he died, I had killed him.

I didn't want the hotcakes now, but I had to eat them. If I walked out and left them, the waitress would notice me some more. She would remember me. "Sure, officer. That's right. A big guy, blond, kind of a scrambled face. Something was bothering him, he acted funny." I ate the hotcakes.

A plane had come in and the limousine was leaving for downtown. I went out and got in it. It made a stop at one of the beach hotels, about five blocks from the apartment building. I left it there and went into the lobby. A later edition of the morning paper was on the stand. I bought one, but the Butler story was unchanged.

I walked the five blocks. The air was fresh with early morning now and there was a faint tinge of pink in the east as I turned the corner at the building. No one saw me. I walked up instead of taking the elevator.

The lamp was still on in the living room, but she wasn't there.

The bottle was on the coffee table, empty. Well, there'd been only about three drinks in it. As exhausted as she was, they'd probably knocked her out. The door to the hallway on the left was closed. She had gone to bed.

I stood looking around the living room. *Had* she gone to bed? You never knew what she'd do. Diana James was dead now because I hadn't known. Maybe she had left. She had a thousand dollars in her purse and she was tough enough, and disliked me enough, to take a chance on it alone just to keep me from getting my hands on the money in those safe-deposit boxes. She'd do it for spite.

I walked softly across the deep-piled rug and eased the door open. Inside it, on the left, the door to the bathroom was ajar, but the bedroom door at the other end of the short hallway was closed. I put my hand on the knob. It was locked on the inside. She was there.

I went back and sat down on the sofa. I took the wallet out of my pocket and removed the three keys. I placed them in a row on the glass top of the coffee table and just looked at them.

I forgot everything else. They were a wonderful sight.

Here it was. I had it made. Nothing remained except a little waiting. The money was where it was perfectly safe, where no one in the world could get it except her. And I had her. When she woke up I'd take that thousand dollars out of her purse so there'd be no chance of her skipping out on me. I should have thought of that before. She couldn't go anywhere without money.

Nobody would ever know I had it. Nobody, that is, except her, and she couldn't talk. There was nothing to connect me with it. And I had better sense than to start throwing it around and attracting attention. They'd never trip me that way. I'd be a long way from here before any of it got back into circulation.

But there were still a few angles to be figured out. I thought of them. What was I going to do with it while I was taking her to California? I had to take her—not because I'd promised, but simply because I had to do it to be safe myself. If I left her to shift for herself once I got the money, she'd be picked up by the police sooner or later, because she was too hot in this area. And if they got her, she'd talk.

But what did I do with the money while we were driving out there? If I tried to take it in the car, there'd always be the chance she would get her hands on it and run. It would take at least five days. Any hour, day or night, she might outguess me and take the pot. She was smart. And she was tough, and she might not be too fussy how she got it back. She could pick up a gun in some hock shop and let me have it in the back of the head out on the desert in New Mexico or Arizona.

No, I had to leave it here. The thing to do was get a couple of safe-deposit boxes of my own, transfer the stuff right into them, and leave it until I came back from the Coast. I could sell the car out there and fly back. It would take only a day to pick it up and be on my way.

I was tired. I put the keys back in the wallet and

shoved it in my pocket. Switching off the light, I lay back on the sofa. Faint bars of light were beginning to show through the Venetian blinds. It was nearly dawn.

I dropped off to sleep....

I was running down a street that had no end. It was night, but there was a light on every other corner. Far behind me somebody else was running. I could hear his footsteps pounding after me, but I could never see him. The single, empty street stretched away to infinity behind me, and ahead. I ran. And when I slowed I could hear him behind me, running. There was nobody, but I could hear him.

I was covered with sweat, and shaking. It was light in the room and little bars of sunlight slanted in through the partly opened Venetian blinds. She was sitting across from me on an overstuffed chair, dressed in her pajamas and the blue robe.

She was smiling. "You moan a lot in your sleep," she said.

Chapter Fourteen

I rubbed my hands across my face. I sat up. The shaking stopped. It was only a dream. But that endless, empty street was still burned into my mind as if it had been put there with a branding iron.

"What time is it?" I asked.

She looked at her watch. "A little after ten."

"How long have you been up?"

"About an hour," she said. "Were you having a nightmare?"

"No," I said. I got off the sofa and went into the kitchen. There was a little coffee in a can in one of the cupboards. I filled the percolator with water, put the coffee in, and set it on a burner on the stove. If she'd been awake an hour it was a wonder she hadn't done something about it herself. But maybe being waited on by servants all your life got to be a habit.

I went back to the living room. "How about taking the coffee off when it's done?" I said. "If it's not too much trouble."

"Are you going somewhere?" she asked, with faint interest.

"I'm going to take a shower. And shave."

She looked at me with distaste. "Perhaps it would help."

I had started for the bathroom, but I stopped now

and turned around. She got a little hard to take, and if we were going to be here for a month or longer we really should work out some sort of plan for getting along together.

"We can't all be beautiful, Your Highness," I said. "So before we go any further, let's get a few things straightened out. You're here because you're hiding from the cops. If they catch you they're going to put you away where you can spend the next forty years scrubbing floors and trying to fight off the Lesbians. This is my apartment. I'm not your servant. I outweigh you by about a hundred pounds. I don't like you. I'd just as soon slap your supercilious face loose as look at you. You can't yell for help because you're not supposed to be in here.

"I may be a little dense, but I just somehow don't see where you're in any position to be pulling that Catherine the Great around here. However, if you do, don't let me stop you. Just keep right on with your snotty arrogance and see what it gets you. Maybe a fat lip would be good for you. How about it?"

She looked up at me with perfect composure. "Are you trying to frighten me?"

"No. I'm just telling you. Get wise to yourself."

She smiled. "But, I mean—you wouldn't try to frighten me, would you?"

I reached down for her. I caught the front of the robe and hauled her erect. We stood touching each other, her face just under mine.

"Maybe you'd like to stand under the shower yourself," I said. "For a half hour or so, in your cute pajamas."

The big eyes were only amused and slightly mocking.

"All right," she said. "But before we do, wouldn't you like to hear the news I heard on the radio?"

"The radio?" I jerked my head around. She couldn't have been listening to it while I was asleep. It was on a table at the end of the sofa I was sleeping on. But it wasn't. It was gone.

"I took it into the bedroom so I wouldn't wake you," she said.

"What news?"

"You're sure you would like to hear it?"

I shook her roughly. *"What news?"*

"That deputy sheriff you hit with the gun isn't expected to live. Who did you say was hiding whom from the police?"

Because I was at least partly prepared for it, it didn't hit me as hard as it would have cold. I managed to keep my face expressionless, and I didn't relax the grip on her robe.

"So what about it?" I said. "In the first place, he's not dead. And it doesn't change anything, anyway. You're still the one they're looking for."

"No, dear," she said. "They're looking for two of us. Your position isn't quite as strong as it was, so don't you think it might be wise to stop trying to threaten me?"

I pushed her back in the chair. "All right. But listen. You're right about one thing: We're in this together. They get one of us, they'll get us both. So you do what I tell you, and don't give me any static. Do we understand each other?"

"We understand each other perfectly," she said.

I took a shower and shaved. I went into the bedroom in my shorts and found a pair of flannel slacks and a sports shirt in the closet. I transferred the wallet into the slacks.

She hadn't made up the bed. Well, that was all right. She was the one who was sleeping in it, and if she liked it that way... Her purse was on the dresser. I opened it and took out the billfold. They were all fifties, and there were twenty-one of them. I took the whole thing out into the living room. She was drinking a cup of coffee.

"Just so you don't decide to run away and join the Brownies," I said, "I'm taking charge of the roll."

Her eyes had that dead, expressionless look in them again. "So you're going to take that too? And leave me without a cent?"

"Relax," I said. "I'm just handling it. For expenses. And to keep you from running out on me. You'll get it back, or what's left of it, when we get to the Coast."

"You're too generous," she said.

"Well, that's the kind of good-time Charlie I am. After all, it's only money."

She shrugged and went back to her coffee.

"I'll be back in a minute with something to eat," I said.

I went downstairs and around the corner to a small grocery. I picked up some cinnamon rolls and a dozen eggs and some bacon, and remembered another pound of coffee. The afternoon papers weren't on the street yet. There was nothing to do but go on waiting. The brassy glare of the sun hurt my eyes. I felt light-headed, and everything was slightly unreal. A police car pulled up at the boulevard stop beside me. I fought a blind impulse to turn my face away and hurry around the corner.

Forty-eight hours ago they wrote traffic tickets, and you said, "Heh, heh, I'm sorry, officer, I didn't realize…No, it won't happen again." Now they followed you through the jungle with their radios whispering, stalking you, and waiting.

When I got back to the apartment she had brought the radio into the living room and was sitting on the floor listening to a program of long-hair music. With a sudden sense of shock I realized this was exactly the same way I'd walked in on her the first time I had ever seen her, and that it had been only two nights ago.

Not years ago, I thought; it had just been days. And we had a month to go.

The recording stopped. She glanced briefly up at me and said, "The tone quality of your radio is atrocious."

"Well, turn it off," I said. "You want something to eat?"

"What do we have?"

"Cinnamon rolls."

"All right," she said indifferently.

I warmed the rolls in the oven and poured some more coffee. We sat down at the table in the kitchen and ate, and then went back into the living room. The radio was still turned on. I went across the dial, looking for news. There was none. It was nearly eleven, however. The afternoon papers should be on the street now.

Then I remembered that the news in them wouldn't be as late as what she'd heard on the radio at ten.

She sat down in the big chair and lit a cigarette. She leaned back and said, "Pacing the floor isn't going to help. Incidentally, how soundproof are these walls and floors?"

I tried to make myself sit still. "They're all right," I said. "I've never heard any of the other tenants. Just be sure you wear those slippers, and don't play the radio too loud."

"Is there anyone who comes in and cleans up? Or has to read the meters, or anything?"

"No," I said. "I had a woman who cleaned up the place once a week, but she quit a month or so ago. And all the gas and electric meters are down in the basement. There's no occasion for anyone to come in here unless we have something delivered, in which case I'll be here to take it. Never answer the door, of course, or the telephone. Nobody'll ever know you're here."

She smiled faintly. "I really have to give you credit. I believe it will work. How long do you think it will be before I can go out?"

"It depends on whether that guy dies or not," I said. "Of course, they're never going to quit looking for you, but normally some of the heat would die down after a while and every cop in the state wouldn't have your picture in front of his eyes all the time. However, that deputy sheriff is going to make it rough. If he dies, they're looking for two people who killed a cop."

"If he dies," she said coolly, "you killed him. I didn't."

"That hasn't got anything to do with it. Nobody

knew I was there. They have no description of me.
Actually, they don't even know I exist. So they have to
get you, to get me. They have descriptions of you, and
pictures. You're real. You exist. They know who they're
looking for. Which brings us right up against the
problem. We might as well get started on it. Stand up."

She looked at me questioningly.

"Stand up," I repeated irritably. "Turn around, very
slowly. Let's get an idea of the job."

She shrugged, but did as I said.

"All right." I lit a cigarette. It wasn't going to be
easy. It was all right to talk about, but just where did
you start? A man could grow a mustache, or shave it
off, or break his nose....

What did you do to camouflage a dish like this?

"A little over average height," I said, more to myself
than to her. "But that part's all right. There are lots of
tall women. But damn few of them as beautiful."

She smiled sardonically. "Thank you."

"I'm not complimenting you," I said, "so don't rup-
ture yourself. This is no game. You're not going to be
easy to hide, and if we don't do a good job, we're
dead."

"Well, you took the job."

"Keep your shirt on. Let's break it down. There are
things we can change, and things we can't. We can
change the color of your hair and the way you do it,
but that alone isn't enough. We can't do anything
about those eyes. Or the bone structure and general
shape of your face.

"You can wear glasses, but that's pretty obvious.
And you can splash on more make-up and widen your

mouth with lipstick, but that still isn't going to do the job."

I was silent for a moment, thinking about it. She started to say something, but I broke in on her.

"Just a minute and then we'll get your ideas. Here are mine. We can't make you plain and drab enough to blend into the scenery because you're too much whistle bait to start with and there are too many things we can't change, so we have to make you a different kind of dish.

"Here's the angle. All the people who are looking for you are men. And since we can't keep 'em from noticing you, we'll make 'em notice the wrong things. We'll start by bleaching your hair up three or four shades. I think we can make it as far as red, or reddish brown. We cut it. You put it up close to your head in tight curls. We may butch it up somewhat, but after we get the groundwork done it'll be safe enough for you to go to a beauty shop and have it patched. You splash on the make-up. Pluck your eyebrows. Overpaint your mouth. So far, so good. Now. Do you wear a girdle?"

She stared coldly. "Really."

"I asked you a question. Do you wear a girdle?"

"When I'm going out, and dressed."

"All right. And how about falsies? How much of all that is yours?"

"Of all the utterly revolting—"

"Shut up," I said. "Maybe there just isn't any way I can get it through your thick head that this is serious. Can't you see what I'm trying to do? You're going to come out a dish, no matter how we slice you, so what we've got to do is make you an entirely different kind of dish. A cheap one. Flashy. If you're not already wearing padding up there, you're going to, and plenty of it. Change your way of walking. Get dresses tight across the hips, leave off the girdle, and let it roll. Cops are men. Who's going to keep his mind on the job and look for the patrician Mrs. Butler with all that going on?"

She shook her head. "You have the most amazing genius for vulgarity I have ever encountered."

"Oh, knock it off," I said. "If you don't like the idea, let's see you come up with a better one."

"You misunderstand me. I wasn't criticizing the idea. It's very good. In fact, it's remarkably ingenious. I was merely objecting to your crude way of expressing yourself, and marveling that someone without even the faintest glimmerings of taste or discrimination could have figured it out."

"Save it, save it." I waved her off. "You can make a speech some other time. Now, if we've agreed on the idea, let's work out the details. We've got to do something about your complexion. Do you tan all right?"

"Yes. Except that I avoid it."

"Not any more. Now, let's see. I could get a sun lamp, except that anybody asking for one at a store here on the Gulf Coast in summer might be locked up for a maniac, so we'll get along without it. This living-room window faces west, and in the afternoon the sun comes in if we raise the Venetian blind. There's no building across the avenue high enough for anybody to see you if you're lying on the floor. Item one, suntan oil."

I got up and found some paper and a pencil and wrote it down.

"Now, what else?"

"Do you have any scissors?"

"No," I said. I wrote that down, and went on: "Home-permanent outfit. Sunglasses. Now, what do I get to bleach your hair with?"

"I haven't the faintest idea," she said.

"You're a big help," I said. "But never mind. I'll get it. Now, can you think of anything else?"

"Only cigarettes. And a bottle of bourbon."

"You won't get tanked up?"

"I never get tanked up, as you put it."

"All right." I stood up. As I started toward the door I stopped and turned. "What banks are those safe-deposit boxes in?"

She answered without hesitation. "The Merchants Trust Company, the Third National, and the Seaboard Bank and Trust Company."

"What name did you use?"

"Names," she said easily. "Each box is under a different one."

"What are they?"

She leaned back in the chair and smiled. "A little late to be checking up now, aren't you? I doubt if they'd answer your questions, anyway."

"No," I said. "I wasn't thinking of calling them. I'm still going under the assumption you had better sense than to try to lie about it, under the circumstances."

"I wasn't lying. The money's in those three banks."

"And the names?"

"Mrs. James R. Hatch, Mrs. Lucille Manning, and

Mrs. Henry L. Carstairs." She named the names off easily, but stopped abruptly at the end and sat there staring at her cigarette, frowning a little.

"What is it?" I asked.

She glanced up at me. "I beg your pardon?"

"I thought you started to say something else."

"No," she said, still frowning as if she were trying to think of something. "That was all. Those are the names."

"O.K.," I said. "I'll be back in a little while."

As I went down in the elevator I tried to figure out what was bothering me. The whole thing was easy now, wasn't it? Even if that deputy sheriff died, they couldn't catch us. She was the only lead they had, and she was too well hidden. The money was there, waiting for me.

Then what was it?

It wasn't anything you could put a finger on. It was just a feeling she was a little unconcerned about giving up all that money. She didn't seem to mind.

Chapter Fifteen

I took a bus across town and got my car out of the storage garage. Both the afternoon papers were out now, but there was nothing new. The deputy sheriff was still unconscious, his condition unchanged. They were tearing the state apart for Madelon Butler.

I found a place to park near a drugstore. Buying a couple of women's magazines, I took them back to the car and began flipping hurriedly through the ads. I didn't find what I wanted. These were the wrong ones, full of cooking recipes and articles on how to refurnish your living room for $64.50. I went back and picked up some more, the glamour type.

There were dozens of ads for different kinds of hair concoctions, but most of them were pretty coy. "You can regain your golden loveliness," they promised, but they didn't say how the hell you got there in the first place.

I threw the magazines in the back seat and found another drugstore. It would be dangerous to keep haunting the same one all the time. I went to the cosmetic counter.

"Could I help you?" the girl asked.

"Yes," I said. "I want one of those home-permanent outfits. And there was something else my wife told me to get but I can't remember the name of it, some kind of goo she uses to lighten the color of her hair."

"A rinse?"

"I don't know what you call it. Anyway, her hair's dark brown to begin with, and with this stuff she gets a little past midfield into blonde territory, a sort of coppery color."

She named three or four.

"That's it," I said on the third one. "I remember now it was Something-Tint. Give me a slip on it, though, just in case I'm wrong and have to bring it back."

I took it back to the car, along with the permanent-wave outfit, and read the instructions. We had to have some cotton pads to put it on with and shampoo to get rid of it after it had been on long enough. I hunted up still another drugstore for these, and while I was there I bought the sunglasses, suntan lotion, and scissors.

That was everything except the whisky and cigarettes. When I stopped for these I saw a delicatessen next to the liquor store and picked up a roast chicken and a bottle of milk, and bought a shopping bag that would hold all of it.

It was one-thirty when I got back to the apartment. The Venetian blind was raised and she was lying on the rug with her face and arms in the sun. She had taken off the robe and rolled the sleeves of her pajamas up to her shoulders. Maybe she had decided to take some interest in the proceedings at last.

"Here." I dug around in the shopping bag and found the suntan lotion. "Smear some of this on."

She sat up and made a face. "I hate being tanned."

"Cheer up," I said. "It's better than prison pallor."

"Yes. Isn't it." She opened the bottle and rubbed some on her face and arms. "Did you get the whisky?"

"Yeah," I said. "Go ahead with your tan. I'll bring a drink."

"Thank you." She lay down again and closed her eyes. The rug was gray, and the long hair was very dark against it.

I unpacked the shopping bag and opened one of the bottles, hiding the other in the back of the broom closet. Since she seemed to be able to handle it without getting noisy, I poured her a heavy one, half a water tumbler with only a little water in it. After all, she was buying it.

I went back into the living room. "How long have you been in the sun now?"

"About fifteen minutes."

"You'd better knock off, then. If you blister and peel, you'll just have to start over."

"Yes." She sat up. I handed her the glass and lowered the Venetian blind.

She took a sip of the drink, still sitting on the floor, and looked at me and smiled. "Hmmm," she said. "You're an excellent bartender. Where's yours?"

"I didn't want any," I said.

"Don't you drink at all?"

"Very little."

She held up the glass. "Well, here's to the admirable Mr. Scarborough. His strength is as the strength of ten, because his heart is pure."

"You seem to feel better."

"I do," she said. "Lots better." She slid over a little so she could lean back against the chair. "I've been thinking about your brilliant idea ever since you left, and the more I think about it, the better I like it. It can't fail. How can they catch Madelon Butler if she has changed completely into someone else?"

"Remember, it's not easy."

"I know. But we can do it. When do we begin?"

"Right now," I said. "Unless you want to finish your drink first."

"I can work on it while you're hacking up my hair." She laughed. "It'll give me courage."

"You'll probably need it," I said.

I spread a bunch of newspapers on the floor and set one of the dining-room chairs in the middle of them. "Sit here," I said. She sat down, looking quite pleased and happy.

The radio was turned on, playing music. "Was there any news while I was gone?" I asked.

She glanced up at me. "Oh, yes. Wasn't it in the papers?"

"What?" I demanded. "For God's sake, what?"

"That deputy sheriff's condition is improving, and they say he'll probably recover."

I sat down weakly and lit a cigarette, the haircutting forgotten. I hadn't realized how bad the pressure had really been until now that it was gone. I hadn't killed any cop. The heat was off me. Even if they caught us, they could only get me for rapping him on the head. Of course, there was still the matter of Diana James, but that was different, somehow. I hadn't actually done that. She had. And Diana James wasn't a cop.

"Has he recovered consciousness yet?" I asked.

"No, but they expect him to any time."

"There's one thing, though," I said. "He recognized you, remember?"

"Yes," she said carelessly. "I know."

"That part won't help," I said, wondering why she was so unconcerned about it.

"Oh, well, they seem to be certain enough that I was there anyway," she said. "His identification won't change anything."

I should have begun to catch on then, but I fumbled it. The roof had to fall in on me before I realized why the news about that deputy sheriff made her so happy.

"Well, Pygmalion," she said, "shall we commence? I'm quite eager to begin life as Susie Mumble."

I was digging through the pile of women's magazines. "There's more to it than a haircut," I said. "You have to learn to talk like Susie."

"I know. Just don't rush me, honey."

I jerked my face around and stared at her. She was smiling.

"You catch on fast," I said.

"Thanks, honey. I'm tryin' all the time." She had even dropped her voice down a little, into a kind of throaty contralto purr. I was conscious of thinking that her husband and Diana James and even the police force had been outnumbered from the first in trying to outguess her.

I found the magazine I was looking for, the one that had several pages of pictures of hair styles. Some of them were short-cropped and careless, and they looked easy. I had a hunch, though, that they weren't that easy.

She was sitting upright in the chair, waiting. I folded the magazine open at one of the pictures and put it on the coffee table where I could see it and use it for a guide. I looked from it to Madelon Butler. The long dark hair just brushed her shoulders.

She glanced down at the picture and then at me with amusement. "You won't find it that simple," she said. "Carelessness is very carefully planned and executed."

"Yes, I know," I said. I took the scissors out of the bag and went into the bathroom for a towel and comb. I put the towel around her shoulders, under the cascade of hair. "Hold it there," I said.

She caught it in front, at her throat. "You'll make an awful mess of it," she said. "But remember, it doesn't matter. The principal thing is to get started, to get it cut, bleached, and waved. Then as soon as my face is tanned I can go to a beauty shop and have it repaired. I'll just say I've been in Central America, and cry a little on their shoulders about the atrocious beauty shops down there."

"That's the idea," I said. I pulled the comb through her hair, sighted at it, and started snipping. I cut around one side and then stood off and looked at it.

It was awful.

It looked as if she'd got caught in a machine.

"Let me see," she said. She got up and went into the bathroom and looked in the mirror. I went with her. She didn't explode, though. She merely sighed and shook her head.

"If you were thinking of hair dressing as a career—"

"So it doesn't look so hot. I'm not finished yet."

"All right," she said. "I'll tell you what you're doing wrong. Don't cut straight across as if you were sawing a plank in two. Hold the comb at an angle and taper it. And let each bunch of hair slide a little between the blades of the scissors so it won't be chopped off square."

We went back and I tried again. I'd left it plenty long intentionally so the first two or three runs at it would just be practice. I cut the other side and evened it up.

This time I got away from that square, chopped-off effect, but it was ragged. It was full of notches up the side of her head. She looked at it again.

"That's better," she said. "And now when you're trying to smooth out those chopped places, the way to do it is to keep the comb and scissors both moving while you cut. Let the hair run through the comb. That way they're not all the same length."

I tried it again. I got the hang of it a little better and managed to erase some of the notches. Then I combed it again and went around the bottom once more, straightening out the jagged ends. We went into the bathroom and took another look at it in the mirror. I stood behind her. Our eyes met.

"It's pretty bad," I said. "But there's one thing."

"What's that?"

"You sure as hell don't look like the pictures of Mrs. Butler."

"Remember, darling?" she said in that throaty voice. "I'm not Mrs. Butler."

"It's a start," I said. I went out and got the bottle of bleach. I handed it to her. "Mix yourself a redhead."

While she was working on it I cleaned up the rug. I rolled the cut-off hair in the newspapers and threw the whole works down the garbage chute.

We were erasing Madelon Butler.

No, I thought; she was erasing Madelon Butler. I had suggested it and started the job, but she was the one who knew how to do it. I could see her already getting the feel of it. She was brilliant; and she was an actress all the way in and out. When she finished the job they'd never find her. The person they were looking for would have ceased to exist. The coolly beautiful aristocrat would be a sexy cupcake talking slang.

It was two-thirty. I tuned the radio across all the stations and found a news program. There was no mention of her or of the deputy sheriff. I wondered if she had been lying. Well, it would be in the late editions.

She came out of the bathroom. She had finished shampooing her hair and was rubbing it with a towel. It was wild and tousled, and she looked like a chrysanthemum. I couldn't see any change in the color.

"It looks as dark as ever," I said.

"That's because it's still wet. As soon as it's dry we can tell."

She raised the Venetian blind again and sat down on the rug before the window, still rubbing her head with the towel. In a few minutes she threw the towel to one side and just ran her fingers through her hair, riffling it in the sunlight.

"I could use another drink," she murmured, glancing around sidewise at me.

"You live on the stuff, don't you?"

"Well," she said, "it's one way."

I went out to the kitchen and poured her another. When I handed it to her she gave me that up-through-the-eyelashes glance and said, "Thank you, honey."

She looked like a chrysanthemum, all right, but a damn beautiful one. And the pajamas didn't do her any harm.

"Practicing Susie again?" I asked.

"Yes," she said. "How'm I doin'?"

"Not bad, considering you're riding on a pass."

She looked up at me, wide-eyed. "What do you mean?"

I squatted down in front of her and ran my fingers up into the tousled hair at the back of her neck. "You're trying to get in free. From what I hear of Susie, she talked like the rustle of new-mown hay because she'd been there and she liked it. But I'd be glad to help you out."

The eyes turned cold. "Aren't you expecting a little too much?"

"How's that?"

"Not even Susie could match your abysmal vulgarity."

"Well, don't get in an uproar. I just asked."

"So you did, in your inimitable fashion. And now if you feel you have received an answer that is intelligible even to you, perhaps you'll take your hand off me."

"This is Susie talking?" I didn't take the hand away. I moved it. It wasn't padding.

"No," she said. She put the drink down on the rug. "*This* is Susie."

She hit me across the face.

I caught both her wrists and held them in my left

hand. "Don't make a habit of that," I said. "It could get you into trouble."

The eyes were completely unafraid. They seemed to be merely thoughtful. "I doubt that I'll ever understand you," she said. "At times you seem to have what passes for intelligence, and yet you deliberately go out of your way to wallow in that revolting crudity."

"Let's don't make a Supreme Court case out of it," I said, turning her arms loose. "It's not that important. If you don't want to put out a little smooching on the side, I'll still live. That you can get anywhere. The geetus is the main issue, remember?"

"You are a sentimental soul, aren't you?"

I stood up. "Baby, where I grew up you could buy a lot more with a hundred and twenty thousand dollars than you could with sentiment."

She said nothing. I started toward the door. As I picked up the car keys off the table, I said, "And, besides, look who's talking."

"What do you mean?" she asked.

"You're the one who's killed two people. Not me."

She stared at me. "Yes," she said. "But even hate is an emotion."

"I guess so," I said. "But there's not much money in it."

I went out and got in the car and drove downtown. I didn't have anything in mind except that I didn't want to get rock-happy sitting around the apartment listening to her yakking. Why didn't she get wise to herself? We were going to be there for a month together; it wouldn't cost anything extra to relax and have a little fun out of it on the side.

But maybe it was just as well, when you thought about it. No woman could ever do anything as simple as going to bed without trying to louse it up with a lot of complicated ground rules and romantic double talk and then wanting a mortgage on your soul. As long as we were mixed up in a business deal and tied to each other for a whole month, we'd probably be better off to go on barking at each other.

I bought an afternoon paper and went into a restaurant and ordered a cup of coffee. "DEPUTY IMPROVED," the headline said. Doctors expected him to recover. He still hadn't regained consciousness.

The rest of the story was the usual rehash, another description of Madelon Butler and the car, and more speculation as to what had become of the money Butler stole. They didn't believe she could have got out of the area with all the roads covered; she must be holed up somewhere inside the ring. They would get her. She was too eye-arresting to escape detection anywhere. And there was the Cadillac. I thought of the Cadillac, and grinned coldly as I sipped the coffee.

There was still no mention of Diana James, but that was understandable. Her body was in the basement, and the whole house had burned down on top of her. It had been only last night. They wouldn't be poking around in the ruins yet. I didn't like to think about it.

I went out. The streets were hot and the air was heavy and breathless, as if a storm were coming up. I could hear the rumble of thunder now and then above the sound of traffic. I didn't have any idea where I was going until I found myself standing on the corner outside the marble-columned entrance. It was the Seaboard Bank and Trust Company.

There was a terrible fascination about it. I stood on the corner while the traffic light changed and a river of people flowed past and around me. It was inside there; it was safe, just waiting to be picked up. In my mind I could see the massive and circular underground door of the vault and the narrow passageways between rows of shiny metal honeycomb made up of thousands of boxes stacked and numbered from floor to ceiling. One of them was bulging with fat bundles of banknotes fastened around the middle with paper bands. And the key to the box was in my pocket.

Two blocks up, on the other side of the street, was the Third National. I could see it from here. Left at the next corner and three blocks south was the Merchants Trust Company. It wouldn't take twenty minutes to cover the three of them. All she had to do was go down the stairs to the vault, sign the card, give her key to the attendant.

People were jostling me. Everybody was hurrying. Two teenage girls tried to shove past me. They looked at each other. One gave me a dirty look and said, "Maybe it's something they started to build here." They went on. I awoke then. It was raining.

I ran across the street and stood under an awning.

Water splashed down in sheets. There was no chance of getting back to the car without being soaked. I looked around. The awning I was under was the front of a movie. I bought a ticket and went in without even looking to see what the picture was.

When I came out I still didn't know, but the rain

had stopped and it was dusk. Lights glistened on shiny black pavement and tires hissed in the street.

Newsboys were calling the late editions. I bought one and opened it.

The headline exploded in my face:

"YOUTH CONFESSES IN BUTLER SLAYING."

It was four blocks back to the car, four blocks of feeling naked and trying not to run.

Chapter Sixteen

Youth confesses.

What about Madelon Butler?

But that wasn't it. That wasn't the big news. If they had caught that blonde and her brother, they had a description of me.

I took the steps three at a time and let myself into the apartment. A light was on in the living room, but I didn't see her anywhere. Then I heard her splashing in the bathroom. I dropped on the sofa and spread the paper open.

I put a cigarette in my mouth but forgot to light it.

Mount Temple. Aug. 6—A startling break in the investigation of the death of J. N. Butler came shortly after 2 P.M. today with the police announcement that Jack D. Finley, 22, of Mount Temple, had broken under questioning and admitted implication in the two-month-old slaying of the missing bank official, whose body was discovered Tuesday afternoon.

Finley, ashen-faced and sobbing, named Mrs. Madelon Butler, the victim's attractive widow, as the mastermind behind the sordid crime.

I stopped and lit the cigarette. It was about the way

I'd had it figured. Finley was the fall guy. I went on, reading fast.

> Finley, who was taken into custody early this morning on a country road some 50 miles southeast of here by officers investigating a tip that a car answering the description of Mrs. Butler's had been seen in the vicinity, at first maintained his innocence, despite his inability to explain what he and his sister, Charisse, 27, were doing in the area. Both had tried to flee at sight of the officers' car.
>
> Later, however, when confronted with the fact that other members of the posse had found Mrs. Butler's Cadillac abandoned at a fishing camp at the end of the road on which they were walking, Finley broke and admitted being an accessory to the slaying.
>
> Mrs. Butler and an unidentified male companion had taken his car at gunpoint and fled early the night before, he said. Police have broadcast a complete description of the stranger.

Well, there it was. I dropped the paper in my lap and sat staring across the room. But it wasn't hopeless. They still didn't have anything but a description. The only person who knew who I was was Diana James, and she was dead.

I started to pick up the paper again. Madelon Butler came in. She was dressed in the skirt and blouse she'd had on last night, and was wearing nylons and bedroom slippers. She switched on the radio and sat down.

Glancing at the paper in my lap, she asked, "Is there anything interesting in the news?"

"You might call it interesting," I said. "Take a look." I tossed it to her.

She raised it and looked at the glaring headline. "Oh?"

"Look," I said, "they just captured your boyfriend. Is that all you've got to say? Just oh?"

She shrugged. "Don't you think I might be pardoned for a slight lack of concern? After all, he tried to kill me. And he wasn't my boyfriend, anyway."

"He wasn't? Then how in hell did he get mixed up in it?"

"He was in love with Cynthia Cannon. Or Diana James, as you call her."

"In love with Diana James? But I don't see—"

She smiled. "It does seem incredible, doesn't it? But I suppose there's no accounting for tastes."

"Cut it out!" I said. I felt as if my head were about to fly off. "Will you answer my question? Or hand me back that paper? I'd like to know at least as much about this as several million other people do by now."

"All right," she said. "I'll tell you." The radio came on then, blaring jazz. She shuddered and reached for the knob. "Excuse me."

She turned the dial and some long-hair music came on. She adjusted the volume, kicked off her mules, and curled her legs up under her in the chair. Lighting a cigarette, she leaned back contentedly.

"Beautiful, isn't it? Don't you love Debussy at this time of day?"

"No," I said. "Which one of you killed Butler?"

Her eyes had a faraway look in them as she listened to the music. "I did," she said.

She was utterly calm. There was no remorse in it, or anger, or anything else. Butler was dead. She had killed him. Like that.

"Why?" I asked. "For the money?"

"No. Because I hated him. And I hated Cynthia Cannon. You don't mind if I refer to her by her right name, do you?"

I was just getting more mixed up all the time. "Then you mean the money didn't have anything to do with it? But still you've got it?"

She smiled a little coldly. "You still attach too much importance to money. I didn't say it didn't have *any-thing* to do with it. It had some significance. I killed both of them because I hated them, and the money was one of the reasons I did hate them. You see, actually, he wasn't stealing it from the bank. He was stealing it from me."

I stared. "From you!"

"That's right. Both of them were quite clever. He was going to use my money to support himself and his trollop. I was to subsidize them. Ingenious, wasn't it?"

I shook my head. "You've lost me. I don't even know what you're talking about. You say this Finley kid was in love with Diana James, and that Butler was stealing the money from you. Are you crazy, or am I? The papers said he stole it from the bank."

She took a long drag on the cigarette, exhaled the smoke, and looked at the glowing tip. "The newspaper stories were quite correct. But I'll try to explain. The bank referred to was founded by my great-grandfather."

"Oh," I said. "I get it now. You owned it."

She smiled. "No. I said it was founded by my great-grandfather. But there were several intervening generations more talented in spending money than in making it. The bank has long since passed into other hands, but at the time my father died he still owned a little over a hundred thousand dollars' worth of its stock. As the sole surviving member of the family, I inherited it.

"Now do you understand? My husband owned nothing of his own, except charm. He was vice president of the bank by virtue of the block of bank stock we owned jointly under the state community property laws. But when he decided to leave me for Cynthia Cannon, he wanted to take the money with him. There was no way he could, legally, of course; but there was another way.

"He merely stole it from the bank. And the bank, after all efforts to capture him and recover the money had failed, would only have to take over the stock to recover the loss. The search would stop. He would be forgotten. No one would lose anything except me." She stopped. Then she smiled coldly and went on: "And I didn't matter, of course."

I had forgotten the cigarette between my fingers. It was burning my hand. "Well, I'll be damned."

She nodded. "Yes," she said. "Aren't we all?"

"But," I said, "if you knew beforehand that he was going to do it—and apparently you did, some way—couldn't you have just called the police that afternoon and had them come out and get the money back and arrest him?"

"Perhaps," she said. "But I resent being taken for a fool. And my patience has a limit. Cynthia Cannon wasn't the first. She merely happened, with my assistance, to be the last. Before her it was Charisse Finley, who worked in the bank, and before that it was someone else.

"I had borne his other infidelities, but when he calmly decided that I was going to support him and his paramour for the rest of their lives, I just as calmly decided he was going to die. After all, when you have nothing further to lose, you no longer have anything to fear."

"But," I said, "I still don't understand what that Finley kid had to do with it."

"That was a little more complex," she said. "He came very near to being a tragic figure, but wound up by being only a fool. He probably regards himself as having been betrayed by two women, both older than he, but the thing that really betrayed him was that money."

"You're not making any sense," I said.

She smiled. "Forgive me," she said. "I keep forgetting I'm talking to a man to whom there is never any motive except money.

"Cynthia Cannon," she went on, "perhaps told you that she was a nurse and that she was in Mount Temple for some seven or eight months taking care of an invalid. The woman she was caring for was the mother of Jack and Charisse Finley.

"That was when Jack Finley began to get this fantastic obsession for her. I don't know whether she encouraged him at first, but at any rate she was nearly ten years older than he was and hardly the type to remain interested very long in being worshiped with such an intense and adolescent passion. I can imagine he was rather sickening, at least to a veteran with Cynthia Cannon's flair for casual bitchiness.

"Anyway, she apparently dropped him rather thoroughly as soon as she began having an affair with my husband. He was older, you see, and less like a moonstruck calf, and she thought he had more money.

"I didn't know any of this until nearly a month after dear Cynthia had left her job in Mount Temple and come back here to Sanport. Then, one Saturday night when my husband was presumably on another fishing trip, Jack Finley came to see me. He was nearly out of his mind. I really don't know what his idea was in telling me, unless it was some absurd notion that possibly I would speak to my husband about it and ask him to leave Cynthia alone. He was actually that wild.

"I began to see very shortly, however, that he was in a really dangerous condition. He had been following my husband down here on weekends, and spying on them, and once had come very close to murdering them both in a hotel room. He had gone up there with a gun, but just before he knocked on the door some returning glimmer of sanity made him turn away and run out.

"I felt sorry for him and tried to show him the stupidity of ruining his life over a casual trollop like Cynthia Cannon, but there is nothing more futile than trying to reason with someone caught up in an obsession like that. He was going to kill my husband."

"I'm beginning to get it," I said. "You had a sucker

just made to order. All you had to do was needle him a little."

She shook her head. "No," she said, a little coldly. "I have just told you I tried to talk him out of his idiocy. It was only when the picture changed and I began to see that it was he and his charming sister that were trying to needle me, as you put it—"

"You're losing me again," I said. "Back up."

She lit another cigarette, chain fashion, and crushed the stub of the first out in the tray. The music went on. The whole thing was crazy. She was perfectly relaxed and at ease and wrapped up in the spell of the music, and the thing she was telling me about was murder.

"All right," she said. "I told you it was somewhat complex. At first it was just a rather stupid young man in the grip of an insane jealousy. It changed later, but he was the one that changed it—he and his sister.

"It was something he let fall that started me thinking. In the course of his spying on them he had discovered that Cynthia Cannon had changed her name. He apparently wondered about it, but didn't attach much importance to it in the overwrought state he was in.

"I did, however, and I arranged a little investigation of my own. She'd changed her name, all right, but I learned several other things that were even more significant. My husband never went near her place when he was meeting her here in Sanport. And on several occasions he bought a considerable amount of clothing for himself, which she took back to her apartment.

"Then I happened to learn that he had let all his life-insurance policies lapse and had borrowed all he could on them. I had a rather good idea by that time as to what they were planning.

"I began, also, to notice a change in Jack Finley. There was something just a little hollow creeping into those tragic protestations that my husband had ruined his life, and mine, and was ruining Cynthia's. He gave me an odd impression of a man who was torn by an insane jealousy, but a jealousy that was under perfect control and was waiting for something.

"Two months of this went by, and I began to suspect what it was. He had told his sister, Charisse. She was slightly more intelligent, and *she* had guessed why Cynthia Cannon had changed her name. And she hated my husband. I think I have already told you that she had been another of his sordid affairs.

"She also worked in the bank. This was important."

She broke off and glanced across at me. "You see it now, don't you?"

"I think so," I said. "Yes. I think I do."

She nodded and went on. "I let myself be persuaded. Our lives were ruined. What more did we have to live for, except revenge? Jack continued to rave about not being able to stand it any longer each time my husband disappeared for the weekend on some pretext or other, but he went on waiting.

"Well, that Saturday noon my husband came home from the bank a few minutes late, and said he was going on another fishing trip. He packed his camping equipment and went upstairs to shower and change clothes. I slipped out, as usual, and searched the car.

"This was the day. I found it.

"It was in a briefcase, rolled up in his bedding. During all those months, while I had been suspecting it and watching, I had often wondered if I would actually go through with it if I ever found the proof and knew, but the moment I opened that briefcase and saw the money there was no longer any doubt or hesitation.

"There wasn't much time. I slipped it out of the car and hid it in the basement, knowing about how long it would take Jack to get there after Charisse had phoned him my husband had been the last to leave the bank and that he was carrying a briefcase.

"He arrived approximately on schedule, coming in the back way on foot. He was quite convincing. His face was white, and his eyes stared like a madman's. He demanded to know if my husband had said he was going fishing again. I told him yes, and perhaps I was just a bit hammy myself. He said we couldn't go on. We couldn't stand it any longer.

"He was still inciting me with this theatrical harangue when I heard my husband coming down the stairs. I took Jack's gun from his pocket and shot him as he came through the door."

She stopped. For a moment she sat staring over my head. Her face showed no emotion whatever.

"All right," I said. "So then of course he took charge of getting rid of the body and the car?"

She nodded. "Yes. He was remarkably efficient and calm. It was almost as if he had planned all the details beforehand. And it really wasn't difficult. The cook wasn't there, as I had been giving her Saturdays off. We merely had to wait until it was dark."

"And what did they do when they found out it wasn't in the car?"

"They both came, Sunday night. And of course I didn't even know what they were talking about. There was no announcement by the bank until Monday morning, you will remember. And certainly *they* had never said anything about money before. I was sure Mr. Butler hadn't had any such sum with him.

"They threatened me with everything. But what could they do? If they actually killed me they'd never find it. And obviously they couldn't threaten me with the police because they were equally guilty. It was somewhat in the nature of an impasse.

"It was buried in a flower bed until the police grew tired of searching the house and watching me. Then I brought it down here and put it in those three safe-deposit boxes."

"And so Finley was actually the one that abandoned the car in front of Diana James's apartment. She swore it was you."

She smiled faintly. "Cynthia, perhaps, wasn't the most intelligent of women, but even she should have known I'd never be guilty of such an adolescent gesture as that."

I sat there for a minute thinking about it. It was beautiful, any way you looked at it. She had out-guessed them all.

Except me, I thought.

I grinned. I was the only one that had won. They had murdered and double-crossed each other for all that time, and in the end the whole thing was three safe-deposit keys worth forty thousand dollars apiece, and I had all three of them in my pocket.

"Baby," I said, "you're a smart cookie. You were almost smart enough to take the pot."

I went downstairs and around the corner. The morning papers were out now. I bought one.

I opened it.

"MRS. BUTLER DEAD," the headline said. "COMPANION SOUGHT."

Chapter Seventeen

I stood there on the corner under a street light just holding the paper in my hand while the pieces fell all around me. It was too much. You could get only part of it at a time.

Somebody was saying something.

"What?" I said. I folded the paper and put it under my arm. There were a half-million other copies covering the whole state like a heavy snowfall, but I had to hide this one. Companion sought. I started away. You didn't run. You didn't ever run. You walked, slowly.

"Hey, here's your change. Don't you want your change, mister?" It was the newsboy. Why did they call a man who was seventy years old a newsboy?

"Oh," I said. "Uh—thanks. Thanks." I put it in my pocket.

I couldn't stand here under the light.

As fast as I got a piece of it sorted out, something else would fall on me. I couldn't stay here. I knew that. The man already thought I was crazy or blind drunk. He was watching me.

But I couldn't go back to the apartment with this paper. If she read it I was through.

I could hear her laughing. I was hiding her from the police for $120,000, but the police weren't looking for her. She was dead. They were looking for me.

I had to do something. Throw it away? With the man standing there watching me and already thinking I was nuts? I looked wildly around for the car. It was parked just ahead of me. I got in and pulled out into the traffic, having no idea where I was going.

I turned right at the corner and went out toward the beach. In a minute I saw a parking place in front of a drugstore and pulled into it. There was light here. I could read the paper sitting in the car.

But even as I spread it open I knew I didn't have to read it. I could have written it. The whole thing would fall into place like the pieces in a chess game in which you had been outclassed before you'd even started to play.

I read it anyway.

It was even worse.

I was right as far as I had guessed, but I hadn't guessed far enough. They had found the body of Diana James, all right. And the deputy sheriff had regained consciousness at last. "Sure it was Mrs. Butler," he said. "I threw the light right in her face. Then this guy slugged me from behind."

Of course they hadn't looked much alike. But they were of the same height and general build, and the same age, and they were both brunettes. There probably wasn't even any dental work to go on, if they called in her dentist. And who was going to?

Nobody was.

Why should they? The deputy sheriff had seen her there, hadn't he? And she had to be on her way *into* the building instead of out, because he had been watching it and nobody had gone in before. Then

there were the shots, after he was slugged. Diana
James had come through the back yard while he was
unconscious. Nobody knew anything about her,
anyway. She'd been gone for six months.

But I had already guessed all that. It had hit me
right in the face the instant I saw the headline.

The thing I hadn't guessed was worse. It was the
clincher. It was that cop at the filling station.

I read it.

*"It was the same guy, all right," Sgt. Kennedy said
flatly. "He fitted the description perfectly. And it
was Finley's car. If we'd only known then.*

*"Sure he was alone, I looked in the car because it
had Vale County license tags. There was nobody
else."*

That was it: "…he was alone."

I had done a beautiful job. I had done such a wonderful job that if she got away and they picked me up
they could hang me.

And all she had to do was walk out the door. She
was free.

I could feel the greasy sweat on the palms of my
hands and the emptiness inside me as I forced myself to read it all. They repeated my description. It
was good. That blonde hellcat had an eye for detail.
She hadn't missed a thing. My eyes caught the last
paragraph.

*"There was something about his face that seemed
familiar," Charisse Finley said. "I keep thinking I've
seen him somewhere before. Or a picture of him."*

I took a cigarette out of my pocket and lit it with shaking fingers. That added the finishing touch. Any hour, day or night, it might come back to her. And I'd never know until they knocked on the door.

That was one I wouldn't read in the papers first.

I tried to get hold of myself. Maybe I could still save it. She might not remember. She hadn't been able to yet; and the longer she puzzled over it, the less certain she'd be. It had been five years at least since the sports pages had carried a picture of me. A thousand—ten thousand—football players had marched across them since then.

I could wait it out. I had to. I couldn't quit. I just couldn't. Hell, the money was almost in my hand. The thought of losing it now made my insides twist up into knots. It would take only a few more days. They weren't even looking for her now; all we had to do was buy her some clothes and have that job on her hair patched up a little. I could give her some story, some excuse for hurrying it. But I had to keep her from seeing a paper for the next two or three days, until she was out of the news.

I sat straight upright. What about the radio?

It might come over the air any minute. Why hadn't I thought of that? But, God, you couldn't remember everything. I hit the starter and shot out of the parking place. When I was around the corner I dropped the paper out in the street. I swung fast at another corner and was headed back to the apartment house.

But maybe she had already heard it. It might even have come over the radio this afternoon while I was gone. How would I know? Did I think she would tell me?

Well, yes, I thought she would tell me. I still had those three keys and that bankroll in my pocket. She wanted those before she left. And there was another thing.

I was the only person left in the world that knew she was still alive.

Maybe she had plans for me. One more wouldn't bother her.

I found a place to park not more than half a block away. I didn't run until I was on the stairs. She wasn't in the living room. The radio was turned off. I closed the door behind me and breathed again with relief. The silence was the most beautiful silence in the world.

I looked quickly around, wondering where she was. I had to do it now; it wouldn't be safe to wait until she had gone to bed. But I had to be sure she wouldn't come in and catch me at it. Then I heard her in the bathroom.

I walked over to the hallway door. It was open, and the bathroom door was open, a few inches. I could hear her humming softly to herself.

"You dressed?" I asked.

"Yes," she called. "Why?" The bathroom door opened wider and she stood looking out at me. She had a towel pinned across her shoulders and was fastening strands of her hair up in little rolls. I could see the difference in shade now. It was definitely lighter, a rich, coppery red.

"I just wondered if you'd heard the news," I said.

Nothing showed in her face. You couldn't read it. She shook her head. "What was it?"

"That deputy sheriff finally came around." I struck a match with my thumbnail and lit the cigarette in my mouth. "And they found Diana James."

"Oh? Well, naturally they would, sooner or later."

"Yeah," I said. "And it was funny. At first they thought it was you."

"They did?" she asked curiously. "But we didn't look anything alike. She—" She stopped and did another take on it. "I see what you mean. The fire."

I had to admire it. If she was acting, she was magnificent.

"That's right," I said. "You see, that deputy recognized you. And somebody heard the shots. So when they found the body there, they naturally thought it was you. But then they found her name engraved inside her wristwatch."

"Oh," she said. You could write your own interpretation. It could mean she believed it, or it could mean she'd already heard the actual news on the radio and was laughing herself sick inside. That was what made it terrible. You might never know for sure until you woke up with a kitchen knife in your throat.

"Well, save the paper," she said carelessly. "I'll read it when I'm through here."

"Oh, damn," I said. "I forgot it. I went off and left it in the lunchroom. But that's all there was."

She shrugged and went back into the bathroom.

She'd be busy there for a few minutes, at least. This was the chance I needed. I went into the kitchen and got a butcher knife out of the drawer. While I was at it, I counted them. There were two of the long ones, one short paring knife, and an ice pick. And the scissors, I thought. Any time I didn't know where all those things were, I'd better start watching behind me.

I shot a glance back into the living room. She was still in the bathroom. I slipped in and picked up the radio off the table. I pulled the cord from the receptacle in the wall. Hurriedly loosening the two screws in back on the underside, I pried up the rear of the chassis enough to get the blade of the knife in under it. I shoved and sliced, feeling wires and parts give way. Then I retightened the screws and plugged it back in. I set it right where it had been before, and took the knife back to the kitchen.

It was about ten minutes before she came out of the bathroom. She had a towel wrapped around her head. She lit a cigarette and stood watching me.

"I don't think my hair will look nearly so ragged as soon as it sets," she said. "And the color came out nicely. Did you notice?"

"Yes," I said.

"It's odd what a change of exterior will do. I feel like an entirely different person. As if I were somebody else, and Madelon Butler were dead."

There was no way to tell how she meant it. It might be perfectly innocent, or she might be very subtly tightening the screws on me. The only thing I knew for sure was that mind of hers was dangerous. I'd seen enough of its work by now.

"Well, that was the general idea," I said.

She sat down, switched on the radio, and leaned back. "Let's see if there's any news."

The radio started to warm up. Then smoke began to pour out of the cabinet.

"Hey," I said, "turn it off! The damn thing's burning up."

She switched it off and looked innocently across at me. "Isn't that odd?" she said. "It was all right a little while ago."

"Must have a short in it," I said. "I'll take it to a shop in the morning and have it fixed."

"Do you think it'll take long?"

"No," I said. "Probably get it back in two or three days."

"That long? Perhaps you could rent one while it's being repaired. Or buy a new one."

"Why?" I asked. "You afraid you'll miss the soap operas?"

"No. I just feel so isolated without it." She smiled. "Cut off from the world, you know, as if I didn't know what was going on."

"I'll tell you what's going on. And you can read the papers."

She'd like hell read the papers.

Again I tried to guess how much she knew. There was just no way to tell. I began to hate that lovely, imperturbable face. Everywhere I looked it was mocking me. It showed nothing. Absolutely nothing. Inside she could be laughing, just waiting for a chance to kill me.

If she knew, all she had to do was wait for me to go to sleep and let me have it. She would have committed the perfect crime. In my pocket were the three keys to all that money, and I was the only remaining person on earth who knew she was still alive. She could walk out, take the money from the boxes, and leisurely board a plane to anywhere she wanted to go.

It could drive you crazy just thinking about it.

I was wanted by the police for killing her, but she could kill me and walk off with $120,000, and nobody would even look for her.

Not for Madelon Butler, because she was dead.

Not for Susie Mumble, because she had been born here in this room and nobody else knew she existed.

It was insane. But there it was.

But did she *know?*

She had probably planned the whole thing the exact instant Diana James had dropped her flashlight there in the basement and we had seen her face as she reached to pick it up. She'd put it all together in that short fraction of a second—the deputy's recognizing her, what would happen if the house burned, all of it.

But, still, could she be sure it had worked? Diana James might have been wearing a watch with her name inside it, as I had said. How could she tell? But I knew by now what kind of mind I was dealing with. For one thing, she could be carefully adding up all these little things: my forgetting to bring in the paper, the strange way the radio had conked out so conveniently.

And, of course, there was always the chance that she had heard the whole thing on the radio during the afternoon. If she had, she was laughing.

I started around the circle again. If she did know, I didn't dare go to sleep. If she didn't know, I had to keep her from learning. That meant she had to stay in here where she couldn't see a paper until she was out of the news, two or three days, or maybe longer.

That, in turn, meant waiting to get at the money, not being able to run. And how much waiting did I think I could take, never knowing from one hour to the next when Charisse Finley might remember who I was?

I could feel the skin along my spine contract with chill at the thought. I couldn't take it. I'd go raving mad sitting here hour after hour just waiting for them to knock on the door. I was even in the phone book. All they'd have to do was drive out here and walk in.

And all the time they'd be hammering at Charisse Finley. Where did you see him? Or his picture? Try to remember. Think. Maybe he was in the papers. About how long ago? Try to guess. A big guy who looked like he'd slept in his face? Maybe he was a pug. Try some pictures of fighters, Joe. How about football players?

We couldn't wait. I had to get out of here. I'd take her down to the banks as soon as they opened in the morning. I'd wear dark glasses and stay in the car, parking as close to each one as possible, making her go right in and out again. She wouldn't have a chance to get at a paper. Not until after we'd got the money, anyway; and afterward it wouldn't matter. Just let her try to hold out any of it or get it back.

I couldn't sit still any longer. I could feel pressure building up inside me as if I were going to explode. I went into the kitchen and mixed two drinks. I'd tell her the plans were changed. But I had to make it sound reasonable, not let her know what I was afraid of.

I brought the drinks in and gave her one.

Then, before I could think of how to start, she glanced thoughtfully at me, frowning a little, and said, "Do you remember asking me about the names those boxes were rented under?"

I had started to taste the drink. Something about the way she said it made me stop. "Yes," I said. "Why?"

She hesitated just slightly. "Well, I...I mean, something has been bothering me, and the more I puzzle about it, the more confused I become. You see, I had it all written down."

"Confused about what?" I demanded.

"The names. I—"

"Look," I snapped at her, "don't try to tell me you've forgotten 'em. You knew 'em this afternoon."

She shook her head. "No. It's not that. I remember them perfectly. But, you see, there are three banks and three names, and now I'm not certain which goes with which."

It was just as if she had read my mind. I held the glass in my hand and stared at her.

Chapter Eighteen

What was she trying to do?

That was what made it awful. You didn't know.
There was no way you could know.

Maybe she had heard the news and was trying to
break my nerve and make me run. But why? If I ran,
and took the keys with me, she'd never get the money.
That couldn't be it.

Maybe she was stalling so we'd be here long enough
for me to break down from sheer exhaustion and
finally go to sleep, so she could kill me. But in that
case, didn't she know that if we waited too long and
the police did get here they'd find her too? Waiting
was just as dangerous for her as it was for me. No, it
was more so, because if they found her here alive I'd
no longer be charged with murder, but she would.

Maybe she did know it but was still cold-nerved
enough to play out a bluff like that until everybody
else had quit. Maybe she was going to let it work on
me, the fear and the suspense and the waiting, until I
was actually afraid to go out on the street where the
cops were looking for me. Maybe I'd crack wide open,
give the keys to her, and ask her to get the stuff out of
the boxes and be stupid enough to expect her to come
back here with it.

Or maybe she was just sweating me a little before

reviewing our contract. Perhaps she wanted to renego-
tiate the terms, using a little pressure here and there.

There were just two things I was sure of. One was
that she wasn't mixed up about those names. Not with
a mind like hers. And the other was that I couldn't let
her know she had me worried.

I took a sip of the drink. "Well, I'll tell you," I said.
"That looks like something that comes under the
heading of your problem. You remember what I told
you? If there was any monkey business about that
money, hell wouldn't hold you. So what are you doing
about it?"

"What do you think I'm doing?" she asked coldly.
"I'm trying to remember. I've been racking my brains
all afternoon."

"And just how long do you think you'll have to rack
'em before you come up with the answer?"

"How do I know?"

I lit a cigarette. "Well, there are two very simple
solutions to it," I said. "The first one is known as the
Blue Method. I just take your throat between my
hands and squeeze it until your face turns the color of
a ripe grape. When you're able to breathe again,
everything comes back to you. It's a great memory aid.
Something scientific about fresh oxygen in the brain.

"The second one is even simpler. As soon as the
banks open in the morning you just pick up the phone
and ask 'em. It's easier on the neck too."

"That would be nice, wouldn't it?" she said icily.
"Just give the bank a list of names, and ask if any of
those people had a safe-deposit box there? You know
they don't give out information like that."

I shook my head. "You don't ask that way. You know how to do it as well as I do, but just to give you an out so we don't have to use the hard way, I'll tell you. Call the Third National. You're Mrs. Henry L. Carstairs. You can't remember whether or not you received a notice that your box rent was due. Would they please look it up? Either they'll say it's paid up until next July, or they'll say they can't find any record of your having a box there. In which case you say you're *so* sorry, you keep forgetting your husband transferred it to another bank.

"Then you call the Merchant's Trust, and try again."

She nodded coolly. "Precisely. And *if* Mrs. Carstairs is lucky, she finds it there. Then one more call to the third bank, using either Mrs. Hatch's name or Mrs. Manning's, will have established all three of them with one call to each bank, no matter which way the last one answers. I know all that. It's elementary.

"But suppose I'm not lucky, and they still say no to Mrs. Carstairs at the Merchant's Trust? We know, of course, by the process of elimination, that she has to be at the Seaboard Bank and Trust. But that still leaves the first two blank, with two names, which means starting around again. One more call, to either of them, will do it, but that may be just one call too many.

"Don't forget that all those boxes are rented under fictitious names, I have no identification at all, my appearance has changed, and I am a fugitive from justice with my picture on the front pages. Anything that makes them take a second look at me when I go in there is dangerous."

She had the answers, all right. She always had the

answers. And she knew I wouldn't tell her she was no longer a fugitive.

"That's right," I said. "But look at it this way. The chances are exactly two to one that you'll find Mrs. Carstairs on the first two calls. Isn't that better than telling me you can't get that money? That way, you haven't got any chance at all."

"You will persist in trying to frighten me, won't you?"

I got up from the sofa and walked across to her. She sat looking up. Our eyes met.

"I've come a long way after that money," I said. "I've taken a lot of chances. I want it. So don't get in my way. I'm not playing any more."

I reached down and caught her by the throat. She didn't fight. She knew the futility of that. The eyes stared at me with their cool disdain.

I intended only to frighten her. But it began to get out of control. I tightened the hands. She'd try to cheat me out of it, would she, the mocking, arrogant, double-crossing little witch?

The room swam around me. She was beating at my arms, trying to reach my face. Make a fool of me, would she? I hated her. I wanted to kill her. My arms trembled; I could hear the roaring of wind in my throat.

Something snapped me out of it just in time. Some glimmer of sanity far back in my mind screamed at me to stop and made me let go of her throat before it was too late. I stood up, trying to control the wild trembling of my hands.

Good God, what had happened? I'd started to go

crazy. I'd nearly killed her. And the only thing on earth that could save me if the police did catch me was the fact that she was still alive. And if I killed her I'd never get that money.

But I couldn't let her know how it had scared me. I turned away and lit another cigarette. When I looked around again she was sitting up, struggling to get her breath.

I was all right now. "That give you an idea?" I asked.

She said nothing until she had recovered and completely regained her composure. She straightened her clothing.

"That's the only language you speak, isn't it?" she said at last.

"It's one we both understand," I said. "Think it over. Maybe you can remember how those names go."

"I'll probably get them straight, in time. But what's the hurry? We have a whole month, don't we?"

"I've changed my mind. This is too close to all those damned cops looking for you. I want to get farther away."

"So you want me to go out on the street while my picture is still on the front pages? Considerate, aren't you?"

"I tell you, we've got to get out of here!"

"And," she went on calmly, "might I remind you of the terms of our agreement, Mr. Scarborough? You were to keep me hidden here for at least a month before I had to go out."

"Listen," I said, my voice beginning to grow loud. "I tell you—" Tell her what? That I was the one the police were looking for?

Maybe she was deliberately trying to drive me crazy.

Suddenly, from nowhere at all, I remembered what that blonde had said. "You'll never get that money. You don't know who you're dealing with. Before it's all over, one of you will kill the other."

I wanted to jump up and run out in the street to get away from her before I went out of my mind and killed her.

Go out in the street? Where every cop in the state was looking for me and had my description?

Sit here, then, with those cool, inscrutable eyes watching me squirm, mocking me? Sit here, waiting hour after hour for the knock on the door that would be the first warning I'd ever have that Charisse Finley had remembered who I was at last?

Sit here and go slowly mad thinking of three safe-deposit boxes stuffed with fat bundles of money being held just out of my reach by this maddening witch?

How long before you broke?

After a while she went to bed.

I made a pot of coffee and watched the hours crawl around the face of the electric clock on the bookshelf. I began to imagine I could hear it. It made a tiny snoring sound. The ashtray filled up with butts. The room was blue with drifting layers of smoke.

I would sit still until my nerves were screaming; then I would walk the floor. Three or four times I heard sirens crying somewhere in the city and each time the breath would stop in my throat in spite of the fact that I knew if they came they wouldn't be using sirens. On a thing like this they came quietly, covered the front and rear exits, and two of them came up and knocked on the door.

It was the elevator that was terrible. The apartment was only two doors away from it and I could hear it, very faintly, if it stopped on this floor and the doors opened. I began to catch myself listening for it. I held my breath listening for it. I imagined I heard it.

Then I would hear it, really hear it, the doors opening softly as it stopped. I waited for the footsteps.

There were never any footsteps because the hall was deeply carpeted. The elevator doors opened and then there was only silence, silence that went up and up, increasing, like a scream.

Which way had they gone?

I waited, counting.

Was it twelve steps? Fifteen? I waited, not even able to breathe now with the pressure building up in my chest, my nerves pulling tighter and tighter, waiting for the knock on the door.

Ten…eleven…fourteen…seventeen…twenty…

They had gone the other way. Or gone on by.

I would be weak and drenched with sweat, a cigarette burning my fingers.

I would relax a little.

Then I would begin listening for the elevator to stop again.

It was morning.

It was Friday morning. This was our last chance until Monday. The banks here were closed all day Saturday in summer.

She came down the hall from the bedroom. She was wearing the blouse and skirt again, and her hair was out of the curlers. It was red, all right, a rich shade of red, in tight, burnished ringlets close to her head, as if the whole thing had been sculptured from one ingot of pure copper.

She smiled. "Pretty, isn't it?"

"Yes," I said, "very pretty. How about those names?"

"My face is a little tanned already, too. Did you notice?"

I stood facing her, blocking her way. "The hell with your face."

Her eyebrows rose coolly. "You appear to be in your usual bad mood. Didn't you sleep well?"

"I slept fine," I said. "I asked you a question. Have you got those names straightened out yet?"

"Would it inconvenience you too much if I had a cup of coffee before you started hounding me about it?"

She had a cup of coffee in the kitchen, black coffee with a slug of whisky in it. I sat down across from her.

"Are you going to call those banks?" I asked.

"Only as a last resort. I'll think about it some more first."

"Don't you know that the more you think about it, the more mixed up you'll get?"

She shook her head. "No. You see, when I wrote them down, with the names of the banks, I remembered the last names came in alphabetical order—Carstairs, Hatch, and Manning—and what I'm trying to remember now is whether the banks actually came in the order in which I went into them. I can almost see the list. It's so tantalizing—at times I'm positive I visualize it exactly as it was."

"Where is the list?" I demanded.

She shrugged. "It was in the house. I forgot to pick it up."

"You forgot!"

"Nobody is perfect." She smiled. "Even the great Mr. Scarborough forgot to bring in the paper he bought."

There it was again, that subtle needling. She knew, all right. She was laughing at me.

I leaned across the table. "Don't stall me," I said. "I can't take much more of you. Are you trying to beat me out of that money?"

"Why should I?" she asked, wide-eyed. "If you carry out your end of the bargain, I can assure you I'll carry out mine."

"All right," I said. "All right. Quit stalling."

"I'm not," she said. "I'm positive that before the end of the month I will have remembered how they go."

I stared at her through a red mist of rage. I wanted to smash that hateful face with my hands.

"Before it's all over one of you will kill the other."

I pushed back from the table, choking.

"By the way," she said calmly, "I thought you were going to take the radio out and have it repaired."

I grabbed up the radio and fled.

It was like one of those dreams where you discover yourself walking out onto a stage naked before a thousand people. The minute I stepped onto the sidewalk I began to cringe. I was not only naked, I was skinless.

I forced myself to walk slowly to the car. When I

was inside it wasn't quite so bad. I drove as if the car were held together with paper clips.

A man was selling papers on a corner. I stopped, hit the horn, and passed him a nickel without looking at him as he handed the paper in. I couldn't look at it now. I drove on, out the beach. The city began to drop away behind me. It was a bright, sunlit day with a soft breeze blowing in off the Gulf.

There were few cars now. I pulled out of the tracks and stopped among the dunes. Opening the paper was like digging up an unexploded bomb.

I looked at it.

She hadn't remembered yet. There was no picture.

But there wouldn't be, I thought. I'd be in jail before they gave the story to the papers.

"MYSTERY SLAYER SOUGHT," the headline said.

There was nothing new. They had just put the story together, with the evidence they had and what Charisse Finley had told them. Mrs. Butler and I had gone back to the house to pick up the money, and as soon as I got it I killed her and set fire to the house in an attempt to cover it up.

It was airtight. How else could they figure it?

I looked around. There were no cars in sight. I got out, carrying the radio, and walked through the dunes toward the line of brush and scrubby salt cedars back from the beach. I threw the radio into it.

"Hey, mister," a boy's voice said, "why'd you throw away your radio?"

I whirled. A boy of ten or twelve had come out of

the bushes carrying a .22 rifle. He walked over to the radio and picked it up.

I looked at him, stupefied. Where had he come from? Then another boy walked out of the tangle of cedar ten yards away. He was carrying a rifle too.

"Hey, Eddie," the first one called. "Lookit the radio. This man just threw it away. Can we have it, mister?"

I tried to think of something. My mouth felt dry. It was ridiculous. The whole thing was insane.

"It's no good," I said at last. "It won't play."

They stared at each other. "Why didn't you have it fixed?"

"I tell you, it's no good!" I suddenly realized I was shouting angrily. I turned and ran back to the car.

I drove carefully and very slowly through the city, fighting every yard of the way against the almost unbearable longing to slam the accelerator to the floor and get back inside the apartment quicker, to pull the walls in around me and hide.

And when I got inside and closed the door I was in a trap. I could feel it tightening. This was where they would come to get me.

And she was there.

She was deliberately trying to drive me mad. Or kill me.

Chapter Nineteen

Friday...

Through the endless hot afternoon I watched her, listening always for the sound of the elevator in the corridor. She lay on the rug in the sun with the sleeves of her pajamas rolled up, and rubbed suntan lotion on her face. After she had tanned for a while she put on the high-heeled shoes and practiced the hip-crawling walk of Susie Mumble. She went up and down the living room before me for hours, working for just the exact amount of slow and tantalizing swing.

She stopped to light a cigarette. "How'm I doin'?" She asked.

"All right, all right. You catch on fast."

"That was a brilliant idea you had," she said. "How do you feel, having created Susie Mumble? Like some great director? Or perhaps as Pygmalion must have felt?" Then she stopped and said thoughtfully, as if to herself, "No, I guess not. Hardly as Pygmalion. He fell in love with Galatea, didn't he?"

"I wouldn't know. They haven't made a comic book of it yet."

"Don't reproach me with that, please. I was nasty. I'm sorry."

So we were having a sweet phase? What was she up to now?

"I'm beginning to feel the part," she said. "And the way to feel it is to live it, as Stanislavski says. I'm not acting Susie Mumble. I am Susie Mumble."

"All right, all right, *all right,* for God's sake, you're Susie Mumble. But while you're swinging it, will you please, for the love of God, try to remember how those names go?"

"Oh, that," she said airily. "I'm sure it'll come back to me in time. Or if it doesn't, in another week or two I'll call the banks, as you suggested."

Another week or two! When she had the steel in you she knew just how to turn it.

She practiced the walk some more. She didn't need to. I tried not to look at how she didn't need to. She could drive you crazy with that alone.

The hours passed as the hours must pass in hell.

It was night again.

I drank coffee and smoked until there was no longer any feeling in my mouth. I turned on all the lights and stood for long periods under the cold shower, slapping myself awake. I listened for the elevator in terror.

How much longer could I go on? Any hour the police might come. There was no way to tell when they might find out who I was. How much longer could I keep from going to sleep? If I dropped off she'd kill me. I could lock myself in the bathroom and go to sleep on the floor, but that would be telling her.

Why didn't I quit? Why didn't I just pick up the phone and tell the police to come and get her? I could run. Maybe they wouldn't even look for me if they had her.

Then I would think of that money again and know I couldn't ever quit. She couldn't whip me. I would stay here and play her war of nerves with her until hell froze over and you could skate across on the ice. No woman ever born was going to cheat me out of that money now, or any part of that money. It was mine. I was going to have it. I'd get it.

I suddenly realized I was saying it aloud, to an empty room.

I dozed, sitting up. At the slightest sound I jerked erect, my heart hammering wildly. I would be drenched with sweat.

Saturday...

I sneaked out to the car once and drove around until I could buy a paper without getting out.

They had found Finley's car at the airport.

"MYSTERY SLAYER SOUGHT HERE."

Charisse Finley still hadn't remembered my name. They had nothing but a description.

But they were closing in, narrowing the field. They were driving me forever toward a smaller and smaller corner.

I began to wonder if I was near the breaking point.

No! I would beat her. I could still beat her.

Though none of it showed anywhere on the surface, I knew it had to be working on her just the same as it was on me. She knew the police were looking for me, and if they found me they found her. God knows what went on inside that chromium-plated soul of hers, but no human being ever born could go on taking that kind of pressure forever without breaking. All I had to do was wait her out. All I had to do was keep her from getting a chance to kill me, and keep myself from going berserk and killing her. If I could sweat it out I could make her break and admit she had remembered how those names went. After all, she must want to run, too.

I watched her for signs of cracking. There were none. There were none at all. She lay with her face and arms in the sunlight and hummed softly to herself. She worked on Susie's speech and mannerisms like an actress getting ready for opening night. She was sweet. And she wasn't worried about anything at all.

The rent on those safe-deposit boxes was paid up for nearly a full year, she said.

Sometime after she had gone to bed I fell asleep. I didn't know when, or how long I slept. The last thing I remembered was sitting straight upright straining my ears for the elevator, and then, somehow, I was lying stretched out on the sofa with that awful feeling of having been awakened by some tiny sound. I jerked my head up and looked groggily around the room, not seeing her at first.

Then I did.

She was slipping silently out into the hallway from the bedroom. She had on that nylon robe, with nothing under it, and she was carrying the scissors in her hand. She was barefoot. She took another soft step and then she saw me looking at her.

She smiled. "Oh. I'm sorry I awakened you."

I couldn't say anything, or move.

She saw me staring at the scissors. She put up a hand and patted the curls that gleamed softly in the light from the single lamp. "I was doing a little repair work on my hair. And I thought I'd slip out to the kitchen and get a drink."

I sat up. I still couldn't find my voice. Or take my eyes from the long, slender blades of those scissors.

She came on into the room and sat down on the floor with her back against the big chair across from me. "Now that I have awakened you with my blundering around," she said sweetly, "why don't we have a cigarette and just talk?"

I watched her with horror. She calmly lit a cigarette and leaned back against the chair, doubling her legs under her. She paid no attention to the fact that she had on nothing beneath that flimsy robe.

"It's nice here, isn't it?" she said quietly.

So I thought I could make her crack? Somewhere deep inside me I could feel myself beginning to come unstuck. I sat still and clenched my jaws together to keep my teeth from chattering. I was shaking as if with a chill.

She opened the scissors, playing with them in her hands. She balanced one slender, shining blade on her fingertip, like a child enchanted with some new toy, and looked from it to me and smiled.

"It's so peaceful. It makes you want to stay forever. Do you remember 'The Lotos-Eaters'?"

Light flickered and gleamed along the blades.

"There is sweet music here that softer falls
Than petals from blown roses on the grass,
Or night-dews on still waters between walls
Of shadowy granite, in a gleaming pass."

She paused. "How does it go? Something about sleep, isn't it? Oh, yes."

She let her head tilt back and watched me dreamily. Smoke from the cigarette in her hand curled upward around the wicked and tapering steel.

> *"Music that gentlier on the spirit lies*
> *Than tir'd eyelids upon tir'd eyes;*
> *Music that brings sweet sleep down from*
>   *the blissful skies."*

She smiled. "Beautiful, isn't it?"

I could feel myself beginning to slip over the edge. I fought it.

It wasn't that I was afraid of a 125-pound woman with a pair of drugstore scissors in her hand. It was that she wasn't human. She was invulnerable. She was unbeatable. Nothing could touch her.

There was a wild, crazy blackness foaming up inside me, urging me to leap up and run, or to lunge for her and tear the scissors away and take her throat in my hands and see if she could be killed.

I hung poised over empty nothing. I slipped a little.

She stood up. "I won't bother you any longer, if you're sleepy," she said. "I think I'll go back to bed."

She knew just how much to turn the screw each time.

Sunday...

Sunday was the slow thickening of horror.

It wasn't a day, beginning at one point and ending at another. There were no days now. Time had melted and run together into one endless and unmarked second of waiting for an explosion when the fuse was always burning and forever a quarter of an inch long.

Midnight came, and I knew I could no longer stay awake. I had to get out. I walked downstairs and around to the car and drove it slowly out of the city and along the beach. When I was far out I pulled off into the dunes and stopped.

I got out. It was black, and the breeze was cool coming in off the sea. I walked five steps away from the car and fell forward onto the sloping edge of a dune. Even as I was falling I was losing consciousness, and the last thing before I blacked out I was running alongside the spinning outer edge of a giant carousel loaded with fat bundles of money and red-haired girls with cool, mocking eyes.

I awoke all at once, like a jungle animal. I turned my head. A car had stopped nearby in the darkness.

A spotlight burst from it. The hot beam swung just above my head and spattered against the side and the open door of the Pontiac. I lay still, afraid even to breathe.

It shifted, searching the ground. He had seen there was no one in the car. The light moved again, just above my head. Then it went off abruptly. I heard a car door open and shut. I held rigid. There was no chance to run. But he might miss me in the darkness.

The beam of a flashlight hit the ground a few feet to my left. He walked forward. He was nearly on top of me now. The beam flipped upward toward the car, and then swung back. It hit me right in the face. I stared into it, blinded.

"What are you doing here?" a voice growled. "You hurt? Or drunk?" Then I heard the sharp intake of breath. *"Hey!"*

I came off the ground, right into the light. He hadn't had time to pull the gun. I caught part of his uniform, pulling him down to me and clubbing for his face with my fist. We were in the sand together. He kicked backward. I followed, swarming over him, wild now, my breath sobbing in my throat. I located his face at last, and swung. He jerked. I held him by the collar and swung again.

I snatched up the light, my hands shaking and dropped it. I clawed it up out of the sand again and flashed it in his face. He was out cold. I ran to the patrol car, jerked the keys out, and threw them far away in the darkness. I heaved the flashlight after them, lunged toward my own car, and fled.

I'd got away from him, but I was just buying time. And there wasn't much more to buy. They would know now that I was here in town.

But even as I gunned the car wildly along the beach in the darkness, I was conscious that my mind was clearing, becoming colder now, and I could think.

An idea began to take shape. I could still win. I could get that money, all of it. I'd beat her yet.

And the way to beat her was to let her think she had won.

It was after five and the sky was reddening in the east when I parked the car a block away from the apartment on a cross street. No one saw me go in. I ran up the stairs. This was the last day. Only a few more hours now and we'd be gone.

No, I thought. *I'd* be gone.

She was in the bedroom. I put on a pot of coffee and went into the bath. I took a shower, as hot as I could stand it and then as cold as it would run, shocking myself awake.

I went into the kitchen. The coffee was almost done. I poured two quick drinks of the whisky and downed them. They burned through five days' accumulation of exhaustion and fear and numbness, clearing my mind. I poured a cup of coffee and lit a cigarette.

I waited. There was no use waking her up. The banks wouldn't open until ten.

At a little after seven I heard her in the bath. In a few minutes she came out. She was wearing the blouse and skirt again. It was odd that with that traveling case she hadn't grabbed up two changes while she was at it.

"Good morning," she said sweetly. "Did you sleep well?"

I walked over in front of her. "Have you got those names figured out yet?"

She gave me a teasing, half-mocking smile. "I'm not absolutely *certain*—"

I caught her by the shoulders and shook her. "Have you?"

"What *is* the hurry, dear? We have the rest of the month."

I turned away from her without a word and walked over to the stove. I poured her a cup of coffee and another for myself. We sat down.

I lit her cigarette. "All right," I said harshly. "You win. What do you want?"

Her eyebrows lifted. "What do you mean?"

"You know what I mean," I said. "You wore me out. I can't take it any longer. We've got to get out. They're closing in on me." I lit my own cigarette and dropped the match in the tray. Then I looked back at her face. "You know they're looking for me instead of you, don't you?"

She nodded. "I suspected it."

"All right. I thought I could wait you out. But I can't. I've taken the heat for four days but I can't take it any longer. One of 'em almost got me out there on the beach two hours ago, and I've had it. We've got to get out."

"Yes," she said quietly. Then she added, "But excuse me for interrupting you. I believe you had something else to say, didn't you?"

"All right," I said savagely. "I did. How much do you want? Half? Don't go any higher than that, because I've still got one thing in my favor. I've got the keys, and if I don't get half nobody gets anything."

She leaned back a little in the chair and smiled. "That sounds eminently fair to me. But did it ever occur to you that possibly there was another facet to it, aside from the money? Remember? It was something I told you."

"What?"

"That I have a deep-seated aversion to being played for a fool. You could have saved yourself all this if you'd told me the news to begin with."

Everybody who wanted to believe that could line up on the right. But I went along with her.

"Well, I'm sorry," I said. "But that's all past now. So the fifty-fifty split is O.K. with you?"

She didn't answer for a moment. She was looking thoughtfully down at her coffee cup. Then she said, "Yes. If we still feel we want to separate when we get to the West Coast, that sounds quite fair to me."

I glanced quickly at her. "What do you mean?"

She raised her eyes then. There was more Susie than Madelon Butler in them. "You don't make it very easy for me to say, do you? But I meant just that. Maybe we won't want to separate by the time we get there."

"It's funny," I said slowly. "I had thought of that too."

There was a faint, tantalizing smile about her lips. "Changing into someone else isn't a thing that happens only from the skin out. I told you I wasn't acting Susie Mumble. I am Susie. And I'm becoming fascinated with her. For the past few days I've been increasingly conscious of unsuspected possibilities in Susie, and I was rather hoping you were too."

Chapter Twenty

I started to get up.

She shook her head, smiling. "No, Lee. Don't rush me. Remember, Susie is something so foreign to my entire life up to this time that I can't hurry her. She has to do her own developing, in her own way. You understand, don't you?"

She stopped abruptly, and before I could say anything, she added, "But enough of this. We've got work to do."

We went in and sat down on the sofa. She was excited now. I put the three keys on the glass top of the coffee table. She separated them, pushing them out one at a time.

"Third National," she murmured happily, "Mrs. Henry L. Carstairs. Merchants Trust, Mrs. James R. Hatch. Seaboard Bank and Trust, Mrs. Lucille Manning."

It was easy now that she had won. Well, almost won. I put the keys back in my wallet.

She looked at her watch. "It's a quarter of eight. The banks won't open until ten. I've got to go to the beauty shop first, and buy some clothes."

I exploded. "Hold it! Don't you realize we haven't got time for that? They know I'm here in town. Every minute of delay is dangerous."

She broke in on me. "Not while you're here in the apartment. And I can't go into those banks like this. My hair may look all right to you, but to another woman it's as ragged as if it had been chewed off. And these clothes are terrible. I look like a ragpicker. People would notice, and that's the one thing we can't risk. I have to look like someone who conceivably might have a safe-deposit box."

In the end I gave in. I had to. As she pointed out, she'd be back by twelve, which was a delay of only two hours. And I didn't want to queer it by starting a fight now.

She called a number of beauty shops until she found one that would take her right away. I gave her two hundred dollars of the bankroll. She called a cab and left.

Just before she opened the door to go out she turned and faced me. That same tantalizing smile was on her face.

"I just happened to think," she said. "When I came in this door I was Madelon Butler. And now I'm going out for the first time as Susie Mumble. Would you like to help me set the mood?"

I helped her. Not that she needed much. The way Susie's mouth felt on mine, they could pour her into the mold any time now. She was a finished product.

She clung to me for a moment. "It won't be long now, will it?"

"No," I said.

It certainly wouldn't.

But it would be long enough.

I walked the floor. I smoked chain fashion. I

listened for the elevator, going through that same old hell of waiting every time it stopped. This would be the time they would come, right at the end when I had it won. In the last four hours.

In the last three hours....

In the last two....

And now, on top of that, I was tightening up just thinking of that trip downtown. That was going to be rugged. The city would be swarming with cops looking for me.

I'd be in the car all the time, though, and that would help. Of course, they had an idea now of what the car looked like, but there were thousands of the same kind and the cop had no chance to see the license plates. The main thing in my favor was the fact that it's hard to tell the size of a man sitting down in a car. And it was my size they were depending on to spot me.

I set the last of it in my mind. I'd tell her we were going to go right on out the highway the minute she came out of the last bank. That would ease her mind as to why I insisted on going along instead of letting her do it alone now that we were all lovey-dovey. But then, at the last minute, I'd think of some reason we had to come back here before we shoved. And when I left here I'd be alone. I wondered if she really thought I was stupid enough to go for that Susie Mumble act. When we had all the money out of the banks, together in one bundle in a suitcase, and I was the last person on earth who knew she was still alive?

The first time my eyes closed I'd grow a pair of scissors out of my throat.

But I had her stopped now.

I went to the desk and wrote out the note to the police. I put the note inside an envelope, addressed and stamped it, and slipped it into the inside pocket of the coat I was going to wear. I'd mail it at some outlying box on my way out of town to be sure it wasn't delivered for at least twelve hours. That would be better than mailing it a day or so later from some other city. That way, they'd know which direction I'd gone.

Twelve hours would do.

If you had $120,000 in your pocket and were no longer being sought for murder, twelve hours' start was fair enough.

When we came back to the apartment all I had to do was take all her clothes, including the ones she had on, and throw them down the garbage chute, and leave her. She wouldn't be likely to go anywhere naked. She'd still be here when the police showed up to collect her.

Of course she would scream her head off and give them a good description and tell them who I was, but they had practically all that already. And the big heat would be off. Even if they caught me, they couldn't lean very hard. Not like murder.

My nerves were so tight now they were singing. I couldn't sit still at all. It was eleven. It was eleven-fifteen. I had to fight myself to get my eyes off the clock long enough to give it a chance to move. Every time I heard the elevator stop I would stand there for an eternity, waiting for the knock on the door.

Then I remembered that when she came back *she* would have to knock on the door to get in. I wondered if I would be able to open it.

She came. It was ten minutes of twelve, and somehow I got the door open.

They'd done a job on her hair. It was like polished copper rings. She was excited and gurgling, carrying a big hatbox and three other bundles.

"Wait till you see me dressed up," she said.

"Hurry it up. For God's sake, hurry."

She disappeared into the bedroom. I waited, feeling my insides tie up in knots. Being so near the end of it made it terrible.

Ten minutes later she came out, walked past me into the center of the room without saying a word, and turned slowly, like a model.

She was Susie, all right. And Susie was a confection, with frosting.

The big floppy picture hat was perched on the side of her head as if it had been nailed to the shining curls. She had on just a shade too much lipstick across a mouth just a shade too wide. The flowery summer dress was short-sleeved and it snuggled lovingly against Susie's natural resources and scenic high points as if it couldn't bear to be torn away. The white shoes were only straps and three-inch heels, and the nylons were ultrasheer with elaborate clocks. She was wearing long white gloves, which showed up the tan of her arms.

Susie was right off the barracks wall.

"Well," she asked coyly, "how do you like your creation?"

"Brother!" I said. Then time came running back and fell in on me again. "Look, I can drool later. Let's get going."

"All right," she said. Then she glanced quickly at my face. "Lee! You haven't shaved."

I'd forgotten that. I'd meant to after that shower, but it had slipped my mind. That was what pressure could do. "Well, the hell with it. We haven't got time."

Then I put a hand up to my face, remembering. I not only hadn't shaved. I hadn't shaved for three days.

I cursed. But there was no use just asking people to stare at me. I ran into the bathroom, yanking off the shirt and tie. While I lathered and scraped I heard her rustling around in the bedroom.

I came out. She was waiting.

"I'll need something to put the money in," she said. "There's a lot of it. Physically, I mean."

"We'll stop somewhere and buy a briefcase," I said impatiently. "No, wait. How about that overnight bag of yours?"

"Certainly. I hadn't thought of that. It'll do nicely, and I'm not taking the old clothes anyway." She went into the bedroom and came out carrying the bag.

I put on the coat, which had been hanging on the back of a chair.

We were ready.

"All right," I said. "Let's go."

When we stepped out onto the street I could feel the skin along my back draw up hard and tight with chill. But by the time we had casually walked the block to the car and got in, it wasn't so bad. I took the sunglasses out of the glove compartment and put them on.

I drove slowly. Traffic was heavy. It was a hot, still day, and I could feel myself sweating beneath the coat.

I watched the traffic lights. I watched the other cars. If we had an accident now...

But we didn't. Nothing happened. Once a squad car pulled up alongside us in the other lane and I could feel my nerves knot up, but the two cops paid no attention to us. They went on past and turned the corner.

We were downtown now, in the thick of traffic. I couldn't turn left into Avalon, where the Seaboard Bank and Trust and the Third National were, so I had to go around the block.

The first time through there wasn't a parking place anywhere in the two blocks between the banks. Next time our luck was better. I found one just a half block beyond the Seaboard. There was a half hour on the meter.

I took out the first two keys and handed them to her. "I'll wait right here while you make both of them. After you come out of the Seaboard, walk on down to the Third National. When you're finished there, walk back this way and stand diagonally across on the corner up there. I'll see you. I can turn left there, so I'll pick you up and we'll be headed for the Merchants Trust."

She smiled, crinkling up her eyes. "Watch Susie's walk," she said. She was as cool as a mint bed.

She got out, carrying the little suitcase.

I watched her. I saw her cross the street behind me. She went up the steps into the bank.

I waited.

My nerves crawled. It was almost physically impossible to sit still. I lit cigarettes. I threw them out after

two puffs. I pretended to be looking for something in
the glove compartment, to keep my face down.
Another patrol car went slowly past in the traffic. It
was a black shark, cruising, deadly, not quite noticing,
easing past, gone. I unclenched my hands.

It was hot. I became aware that I was counting. I
didn't know what I was counting; I was just saying
numbers. I tried to follow her in my mind. Where was
she now? She had to go through the bank to the rear,
down the steps, through the massive doorway. She
signed the card, she gave her key to an attendant in
the shiny corridors between walls of steel honeycomb.
Now she was going into one of the booths, closing the
door, sliding the lid off the box, transferring the money
to the overnight bag, coming out....

Up the steps, through the bank, out the doorway,
down the steps outside....

I stared into the rear-view mirror.

There she was.

She came out. She flowed down the steps with the
sexy indolence of Susie and sauntered across the street
behind me. She came up the sidewalk, and as she
passed the car she turned her face and smiled. One
eye closed ever so slightly in a wink.

One away.

I waited again. I was watching the parking meter
now. It was getting close. I wished I had asked her to
put a nickel in it. If the flag dropped I had to get out
and do it. I didn't want to get out. I felt in my pocket.

I didn't have a nickel.

I watched the meter. Sweat ran slowly down my face.

It had three minutes left on it when I saw her cross

the street ahead of me and stand on the corner, waiting.

I picked her up. My shirt was wet. My hands trembled. I couldn't wait for her to get the door closed. "Did you get it?" I demanded. "Was it all right? Did you have any trouble?"

She laughed softly. "Not a bit. Take it slowly, so you'll miss that next light. I want to show you something."

The light caught us. I stopped. "Open it," I whispered. I felt as if I were being strangled. "Open it!"

She had the overnight bag in her lap. She unsnapped the two latches, smiling at me out of the corners of her eyes. "Look."

She raised the lid just a couple of inches. I looked in. I forgot everything else. It was worth it. It was worth everything I had gone through. It was beautiful. I saw twenties, fifties, hundreds, in bundles. In fat bundles girdled with paper bands.

I wanted to plunge my hands into it.

"Watch," she whispered. She slid a white-gloved hand in under the lid and broke one of the bands and stirred the loosened bundle with a caressing slowness that was almost sexual. I watched, gripping the wheel until my fingers hurt.

She snapped the lid shut. I took the other key out of my wallet and gave it to her. We were still waiting for the light. When she had put the key in her purse I reached over and took her hand. I squeezed it. She squeezed back.

"Look," I whispered, "after we've finished this last one, let's go back to the apartment. Just for a few minutes, before we start. Susie wouldn't mind, would she?"

She gave me a sidelong glance and said, "I don't think she would. Not for just a few minutes."

She had slid the bag back a little in her lap and she was straightening the seams of her stockings, doing it deliberately and very slowly, one long lovely leg at a time. She turned her face just slightly so her eyes were smiling obliquely up at me from under the curving lashes.

"After all," she said softly, "it was Venus, wasn't it, who breathed life into Galatea?"

It was wonderful. Oh, Lord, it was wonderful.

I could hardly hear her now. The whisper was tremulous, catching in her throat. "This is shameless, isn't it? In brilliant sunlight, in the middle of town. I— I think Susie is going to be a revelation to both of us. Oh, won't that light ever change?"

If she didn't shut up and stop it I'd go crazy right there in the street. I had to look away from her.

It was terrific. If you lived twenty consecutive lifetimes you'd never run across anything quite like it. I almost missed the light, just thinking of the beauty of it.

She had outguessed them all, and she thought she had outguessed me. And now we were going back to the apartment, we were going to launch the tremulous and smoldering Susie, and I was going to walk out when it was done with $120,000 I'd never have to divide with anybody. And not only that. The thing that made it an absolute masterpiece was the fact that now I wouldn't even have any battle to get those clothes so I could throw them down the garbage chute. She'd help me. She'd help me all the way.

You would never beat it. You would never approach it again.

Horns were blasting behind us. I snapped out of it.

The street the Merchants Trust was on was one of the main drags, and I couldn't turn left into it either. I had to go around the block again.

We were shot with luck. A man pulled out of a parking place less than fifty feet beyond the ornate, marble-columned entrance. I slid into it. She patted my hand and got out.

I turned my head and watched her. I watched the slow, seductive tempo of Susie's walk. She went along the sidewalk in the sun looking like something the censors had cut out of a sailor's dream. She went into the bank.

It was only a few minutes more.

I tried to light a cigarette. My hands shook. A cop came by on a motor tricycle, looking at meters. My whole back turned to ice. He went on, not even looking at me. I breathed again.

I set the rear-view mirror so I could watch the entrance without craning my neck. I put my hands down on the seat and clenched them tightly to stop the trembling. It was being so near that made it awful. I thought of the money. I thought of the apartment bedroom, the Venetian blinds drawn, and Susie. I tried to quit thinking of both, before I exploded.

It had to be less than five minutes now. She'd been gone—how long? I didn't know. Time had lost all meaning. The whole world was holding its breath.

Then I saw her.

She came out of the bank. She walked down the

steps and diagonally across the sidewalk toward the car. I could feel the sigh coming right up from the bottom of my lungs.

It was made now. There was only that short drive back to the apartment. I started the motor and reached out a hand to open the door for her. She saw me watching her, and smiled.

But she didn't stop.

She went right on by. The white-gloved left hand, which was carrying the purse down beside her thigh, made a little gesture as she went by the window. Three of the fingers waved.

Good-by!

I lunged for the door handle. Then I stopped, the absolute horror of it beginning to break over me. I was sick. I couldn't move. I was empty inside, and cold, and somewhere far back in the recesses of my mind I thought I could hear myself screaming. But there was no sound except the traffic and the shuffle of feet along the sidewalk.

She went slowly on down the street, her hips swaying.

I didn't know what I was doing now. I yanked the wheel and lurched out of the parking place. A car behind almost hit me. The driver slammed on his brakes and leaned out to curse me. I was out in traffic. Everything was unreal, like a bad dream. I was abreast of her. I hit the horn. She strolled casually on. Somebody else turned and looked. I cringed. I wanted to hide.

I crawled ahead. Cars behind me were honking. I came to the corner. The light was red. I stopped. She stopped on the sidewalk in the crowd waiting for the light. I beeped the horn, hesitantly, timidly. It roared.

She turned her face slowly and glanced in my direction, cool and imperturbable and utterly serene. I formed the words with my mouth: Please, please, please...Her gaze swept on.

The light changed. She stepped off the curb. I started across the intersection. Then she stepped back on the sidewalk, and turned right, down the cross street. I had gone too far into the intersection to turn. I turned anyway.

I was being engulfed in madness. Everything was distorted, and dark, and wild, and I had the sensation of being caught and buffeted by some howling wind. My left fender raked the fender of a car stopped at the crosswalk for the light. A whistle shrilled. I swung on around. I crashed against the side of the car that had made the right turn inside me.

Whistles were blowing everywhere. I saw a cop running toward me from the opposite corner. I slammed ahead, tearing a fender from the car on my right. Both lanes were blocked by cars stopped for the light at the next corner. I saw her walking coolly along the sidewalk.

I slammed on the brakes and lunged for the door. I was out in the street. Two cops in uniform were coming down on me. Men jumped from both the cars I had hit. The whistles were blowing again. I lunged toward the curb. Running men were crashing into me, trying to hold me. But now it all faded away, and I could see nothing except her. There was nothing else in the world except a foaming, dark madness, and

Madelon Butler walking serenely along the street, going away. She had the money. And if she got away they'd hang me. I was shouting. I was trying to point. I was raging.

"Madelon Butler! That's Madelon Butler!"

Nobody listened. Nobody paid any attention.

Couldn't they see her?

Hands were grabbing me. Arms tightened about my neck and around my legs. I felt the weight of bodies. Everybody was yelling. A siren wailed shortly and ground to a stop somewhere behind me. Half-seen faces bobbed in front of me and I swung my fists and they disappeared, to be replaced by even more. I plowed on. I went on toward the curb, taking them with me. She was nearly abreast. I could see the coppery curls glinting in the sunlight and the slow, seductive roll of her hips and thighs the way she had practiced it, and the small overnight bag with $120,000 in it swinging gently in her other hand.

Something landed on my head and knocked me to my knees. I got off the pavement and went between two parked cars and up onto the curb, peeling them off behind me like a bunch of grapes pulled through the slats of a Venetian blind.

"Stop her! Stop her! Stop Madelon Butler stop madelon butler madelonbutler—"

They went around and over and piled onto me again. Nobody could shoot. Saps were swinging and I could feel them just faintly, like rain falling on my head and shoulders as I fought, and fell, and crawled toward her.

She sauntered past just as we got up onto the sidewalk, swinging wide to avoid the seething whirlpool of us, and just after she had gone by she turned her face and looked around, right into mine, her eyes cool and patrician and just faintly curious. Then she picked up the lazy beat of Susie again and went on.

Saliva ran out of my mouth. I was screaming. I could hear myself. Somewhere above the sound of the blows and the cursing and the mad scraping of shoes against pavement and the gasp of labored breathing and the crash of splintering glass as somebody sailed into a store window I could hear myself screaming.

Blood was running down into my face. Just before I went down for the last time under the sea of bodies I saw her again.

She was at the corner. With one last swing of her hips she went around it and she was gone.

Chapter Twenty-one

I'm not crazy. I tell you I'm as sane as you are.

Listen.

I tell you Madelon Butler is still alive. Alive, you understand? *Alive.* She's out there somewhere. She's laughing. She's free.

And she's got $120,000.

Why do I think she's got it? *Why?* Look. When hell freezes over and you can skate across the Styx she'll still have it. Five people tried to take it away from her, and now two of us are dead and two are in the state prison and I'm in here with these people. That's why she's got it.

They could find her if they'd look and quit just shaking their heads when I try to tell them she's still alive. She's a redhead now, and God knows what her name is, and she looks like something on a barbershop calendar and walks and talks like all the itch since Eve, but she's Madelon Butler.

They sweated me for twenty-four hours after they brought me in while I sat under a big light and they walked around in the dark outside it asking questions, questions, questions, one after the other, hour after hour, sometimes one man, sometimes two, and sometimes three of them at once asking me what I had done with the money until I finally quit begging and pleading and yelling for them to block the airport and the railroad stations and the bus depot so they could catch her before she got away, until I finally just gave up and went to sleep with them barking at me. I went to sleep sitting under a big white light on a stool.

I knew she was gone by then. But I could still prove I hadn't killed her.

Sure I could.

They finally got a lawyer for me and I told him so many times he began to believe me. He got the police to send some men out to the apartment so they could see for themselves she had been there. The lawyer went along and they took a photographer and a finger-print man from the lab.

Her robe and the pajamas and those fur-trimmed slippers weren't cheap stuff. They could be traced back to the store where she had bought them. That would convince the knuckleheads that the girl who'd been there in the apartment wasn't just any girl, but Madelon Butler herself.

The only trouble was there wasn't anything there.

Nothing. Absolutely nothing. The pajamas and the robe and the slippers were gone. The boxes her other clothes had come in were gone. There wasn't a cigarette butt with lipstick on it, or a single fingerprint on the whisky bottles or any of the glasses. There wasn't a trace of lipstick on a towel or a pillow, nothing left of the permanent wave outfit, or even the bottle of bleach.

It went into the court record just the way they said it when they came back.

There hadn't been any girl in that apartment.

I began to see it.

She couldn't have gone back there after she had ditched me, because she had no key to get in. She had done it before we came downtown, while I was shaving. She had cleaned up, and she had thrown all her clothes down the garbage chute.

Well, that was what I was going to do, but she just beat me to it.

They found the letter in my coat, the one I'd never had a chance to mail. They asked me if that was right, that I was hiding Madelon Butler in my apartment to keep the police from finding her but that I'd written them a letter telling them where she was.

I tried to explain it. But the deal about the money loused up everything.

That was the reason they wouldn't go for a court order to exhume the body of Diana James for identification. The thing about the money had already convinced them I was mad.

That and a few other things.

The trouble was that *nobody* had ever seen Madelon Butler again after that instant the cop had flashed his light on her face on the lawn behind the house, just before I slugged him. Charisse Finley testified that Madelon Butler and I had left the fishing camp together and that it was a foregone conclusion, with two such people as us after the same thing, that one would kill the other before the day was over. The other cop and the kid in the filling station testified that I'd been alone when I came through that little town four hours after the fire. So there it was.

But that wasn't even half of it.

The cop who had jumped me out on the beach testified he had found me sleeping on a sand dune at five o'clock in the morning.

Two traffic cops, two patrol-car crews, and three plainclothes men testified it took the seven of them plus the drivers of the two cars I'd hit to subdue me after I'd gone berserk in traffic under the delusion I had seen Madelon Butler walking along the curb. I was big, but I wasn't that big. I was a maniac.

They rounded up twenty witnesses and every one of them said there hadn't been anybody there that looked anything at all like Madelon Butler. I pleaded. I raged. I described her.

Eight of them said sure, they'd seen the cupcake in the big hat, and that if I thought *she* looked anything like Madelon Butler there was no hope for me. Four of them were women, who'd been looking at her clothes. And there was no point in even asking the men what they'd been looking at.

Then those two kids who had seen me throw away the radio told the court that when they took it to a repair man he'd said the only way he could figure it had got in the mess it was in was that somebody had stabbed it with a knife. The repair man repeated it under oath.

Driven mad by guilt, they said. I had stabbed the radio because it kept talking about the woman I had killed. And I had been sleeping out on the beach because I was suffering from a delusion she was there in my apartment. Then I had finally blown my stack downtown in the traffic in broad daylight because I had reached the point where any woman was beginning to look like Madelon Butler to me.

But that still wasn't it. It was the money.

This was after they had come back from that trip to the apartment, and they were already beginning to shake their heads while they listened to my raving, if they listened at all. But when I told them for the fiftieth time what I was doing downtown, and about the banks, and how she'd run out on me after getting the money out of the last one, they said they'd check it out.

And they said this was going to be the last, if it was as crazy as the rest. They were getting tired of it. But that was all right. I knew I had them this time.

They investigated. They got sworn testimony from all the vault employees in all three banks.

No boxes had ever been rented to Mrs. Henry L. Carstairs, Mrs. James R. Hatch, or Mrs. Lucille Manning. They had never even heard of the names. And no woman even remotely answering the description I gave them had ever come into any of the vaults that day.

But, they said, Mrs. Madelon Butler herself, as president of the historical society she had founded, had had a box in each of the banks for years for the storage of documents and family papers.

When they came back and told me that, they had to call the guards.

And sometimes even now I can feel it boiling around there inside me, that yell or scream or laugh or whatever it is, when I think that for four days and nights that $120,000 was there in the bedroom of my apartment, either in that little overnight bag or under the mattress of the bed.

She'd had it all the time. But she really hadn't heard the news over the radio before I butched it up, and she wasn't completely sure she was off the hook until I told her. She had a good idea she was, but she wanted to be certain, and she wanted to finish the job on Susie Mumble before she scrammed.

And maybe...

But that's why I wake up screaming.

Maybe she was on the level with that Susie Mumble play for me. It would add up that way, too. Maybe she did want the two of us to go away together, but she didn't want me to know she had been lying about the banks and had to go through with the act of getting it out.

That's it, you see. I'll never know. There's no way I can ever know. Because she could very easily have seen that letter addressed to the police in the pocket of my coat while I was shaving.

It figures, all right. It checks out with the way she did it there at the end. That first bank, the Seaboard Trust, is on a corner, and she could merely have gone on out a side door and left me waiting there in the car forever. It would have been easier that way, and less dangerous. But if she had seen that letter to the police? She wanted me to have a good look at that money and one last, lingering glimpse of the potentialities of Susie Mumble, so I'd have something to remember in case I ever find it dull around this place.

You see why I wake up that way? It's a dream I have. I'm sitting there in the car watching her come out of that last bank and swing toward me across the sidewalk in the sun with the coppery hair shining and that tantalizing smile of Susie's on her face and all that unhampered Susie running loose inside that summer dress, seeing her and thinking that in only a few minutes we'll be in the apartment with the blinds drawn, in the semigloom, with a small overnight bag open on the floor beside the bed with $120,000 in fat bundles of currency inside it and maybe one nylon stocking, a sheer nylon with clocks, draped carelessly across one corner, as if it had been dropped hurriedly by someone who didn't care where it fell....

And then in this dream she waves three fingers of her left hand and saunters on down the street, past me, and she's gone, and I'm trapped in a car in traffic at high noon in the middle of a city of 400,000, where two hundred cops are just waiting for me to step out on the street so they can spot me. I wake up.

Scream?

Who wouldn't?

**And Coming Soon From
HARD CASE CRIME!**

Say It With Bullets
by RICHARD POWELL

Bill Wayne was supposed to be on a bus tour of the West—but he was really on a mission to find out which of his old army buddies shot him in the back and left him for dead.

Witness to Myself
by SEYMOUR SHUBIN

Tormented by memories of a day from his past, Alan Benning returns to the scene of his crime—to try to figure out just what he is guilty of.

Bust
by KEN BRUEN and JASON STARR

A businessman having an affair with his secretary discovers that secrets can kill in this first-ever collaboration between the award-winning authors of *The Guards* and *Twisted City*.

The Last Quarry
by MAX ALLAN COLLINS

In the first new Quarry novel in more than a decade, Collins gives his hit man hero an assignment that may be the last one he'll ever get.

**To order, visit www.HardCaseCrime.com or call
1-800-481-9191 (10am to 9pm EST).**
Each title just $6.99 ($8.99 in Canada), plus shipping and handling.